EDITOR KILL FEE

BY

G.G. COLLINS

Chamisa Canyon Publishing
chamisacanyon@live.com
Attn: Rights & Permissions

Book Cover by Vila Design
Editing by Jay Terre

ISBN 978-1-7354282-3-9
ISBN 978-1-7354282-2-2 (eBook)

Books by G.G. Collins

Reluctant Medium
Lemurian Medium
Atomic Medium
Anasazi Medium
Presence: A Rachel Blackstone Paranormal Mystery Short Story
Dead Editor File
Looking Glass Editor
Editor Kill Fee
Murder USA: A Crime Fiction Tour of the Nation
(Contributor)
Flying Change
Without Notice

Forthcoming:
Skinwalker Medium

For Pam & Olivia

Best friends.

"Book publishing would be so much easier without authors."

– Dan Brown, American Author

Chapter 1

Anita Juárez was going to be late to chair the Santa Fe Wine and Crime mystery readers group. She was current president of the club, even though she lived in Pecos, to the southeast of the capital city. The office needed her to finish some last-minute press releases promoting the Pecos National Historical Park where she worked. She had reluctantly agreed to work later than planned. Now it would be a struggle to make her meeting.

Their guest speaker this week: Taylor Browning, the mystery editor at Piñon Publishing. Anita had to be there to introduce her. As president, it was her responsibility to invite interesting and informative speakers. Taylor had emailed her bio and a discussion synopsis. It promised to be an interesting tutorial about book publishing. Along with her remarks, she promised to bring show-and-tell items that told the journey of a book from manuscript to bookstore. The club members would love it.

Distracted, she'd missed her turnoff to Interstate 25. Anita continued until she bounced over a cattle guard. Jarred from her thoughts, she realized her location.

"Oh no!" she said in disgust. "I can't believe I did this."

She found herself on 63A, a forest road that leads to an abandoned fire lookout tower called by some, the Devil's Tower. More alarming, her sudden awareness she was driving the legendary road. It was famous – more infamous – for good reason. Several people had disappeared in this area.

"I'll look for a turn around when I get the chance," she mumbled to herself.

She passed a bicyclist who peddled back to town. He stopped to let her pass and waved. Anita didn't notice him; she was absorbed in finding a good place to make a U-turn.

The road was drivable at first, but as she progressed it became rutted and steep. Eventually she knew it was all but impassable. Only the most off-road worthy 4-wheel drive vehicle could hope to reach the end. At least, that is what she'd heard, having never ventured out this way. She regretted her bout of highway hypnosis that had put her on this unscheduled excursion.

After about fifteen minutes of axle-breaking bumping and grinding, Anita found a spot wide enough to turn the car around, if she could avoid the deep ditches. With a sigh of relief she turned her white Honda as far as she dared, and then backed up. Certain she would clear the ditch, she accelerated slowly. Maybe she would only be a few minutes late for the meeting after all.

The radio stopped playing and the dash lights went out. Despite turning the steering wheel, the car was still headed straight for the ditch! Even with a hard left, the car wasn't responding. An abrupt coldness settled over her. Maybe there was a front coming through.

Anita applied the brakes to no avail. The car slid on gravel along the edge of the road causing her stomach to lurch. Turning was futile and she momentarily wondered why she still had her hands clenched on the wheel if it was not responding. With a lurch, the passenger side front wheel fell sharply into the ditch. Anita tried repeatedly to start the vehicle, but it was pointless. Nothing but unfriendly sounds churned from the engine.

"Well, that's that," she said.

She took a quick look around the interior of the car. Her meeting notes had slid out of the manila envelope. The list of expected guests the members were bringing rested on the floor mat. Reaching for it strained her shoulder strap so she unfastened the belt. When she had the list in her hand, she saw *that* name again. It seemed to pulsate on the page.

"Why our meeting?" she demanded from the silence.

She had circled the offending name at home. Next to it she had written, "NO!"

"How dare he show up at her club?

Anita could feel the knot in her stomach she noticed when something distasteful or frightening emerged in her life. Maybe her car getting stuck wasn't the worst thing that could happen. At least, she'd miss that encounter.

With a shove, she opened the driver's door. The crazy angle of the car made the effort an uphill battle. Once out, she walked around the front of the car to look at the damage. It was going to be a long walk back to Pecos. This quandary would require a tow truck with a winch. The right front tire was wedged between the walls of a deep trench euphemistically called a ditch.

What a wretched angle. Front-end work would be necessary. The dollar signs accumulated in her mind; she didn't want to calculate the sum. Repairs would be bad for her budget.

I'll get my purse and head back, she thought. I can probably be home shortly before dark. I'm not afraid of a little walking.

Before she could retrieve her things, something stopped her. The silence was complete; not even a bird sang. It, whatever it was, seemed almost palpable, but not visible. Motionless like a startled deer, she listened intently. In the distance something cried an eerie high sound. She didn't recognize it, but thought it too far away to be dangerous.

"Whatever is that?" she whispered. "And when did I begin talking to myself?"

Concerned but not afraid, she tried again to return to her car, but she couldn't seem to move her feet in that direction. Anita looked around her and saw only trees, but something seemed to move in and around them. A miasma undulated in the forest. It was mostly clear but seemed to have folds mixed in. It reminded her of rumbled plastic wrap. But what could it be?

An unease settled over her as it approached. The closer it came, the more alarmed she became. And still, she couldn't move. It reached her and wrapped around her. She felt entrapped and a short of breath. It seemed to be squeezing her gently, constricting her movement.

Now, she was frightened. She wondered if the people who had disappeared from this area had the same experience. Before she could consider this further something caught her attention, she looked up and appeared to listen.

Anita stood on Devil's Road under a perfect blue sky and nodded, as though in agreement. That's when she felt pulling. She was at its mercy as she walked to the side of the road, cautiously stepped over the ditch, steadied herself against a tree and disappeared into the forest along with the mysterious haze.

Chapter 2

Taylor Browning walked the couple of blocks to the library under the same perfect azure sky Anita had experienced. The air was warm and dry. She could still see the ski runs to the northeast of Santa Fe on Mount Baldy. The Sangre de Cristos were alive with pine and aspen. She could almost hear the heart-shaped leaves quaking in the wind. Soon, the Sangres would exchange the green for gold, but not until the last chile harvest. Visitors came from all over to take part in the New Mexico autumn burst of gold and the Albuquerque Balloon Fiesta, but Taylor liked the newly minted spring leaves equally well. There was something magical about starting over every year.

She entered the downtown library, located on the same street as Piñon Publishing. It had been a short walk. As she entered the library meeting room, she noticed the club members gathering around the refreshment table instead of starting the meeting.

The snack table weighed heavily in doughnuts, bear claws, nuts and the ubiquitous chips and salsa. Two percolators held coffee and tea; the larger held tea because this group of mystery lovers was heavy on the cozy reading side. If the library allowed them, she was certain there would be cats in the audience as well.

But today, everyone seemed to be holding wine glasses. It was after all the Wine and Crime book club. Taylor sensed a general mood of apprehension; definitely out of the ordinary.

One of the members approached her, smiling and shaking her hand.

"Hi Taylor. I'm Rebecca, club vice-president. I'm sorry, Anita hasn't arrived as yet."

Taylor remembered Rebecca from her other visits to the group. A tall woman, she had joined the club after retiring to New Mexico.

"I'm sure she'll be along," Taylor said.

"Thing is," Rebecca added. "We've tried to call her, but she's not answering her cell. We're a little worried."

"How late is she?"

"Normally, we'd be introducing you about now, after the business meeting."

"Why don't I go ahead and do my thing," Taylor said. "I'm sure she'll show up."

But she didn't. Taylor finished her presentation to a restless crowd. There was interest in bluelines, book cover proofs and galleys but everyone also watched for Anita to arrive. Her presentation completed; Anita was still MIA. Some of the members were clearly worried as they spoke softly in small groups. Frequent glances at the door still didn't produce Anita.

As Taylor packed up her show-and-tell, Rebecca approached her again.

"I'm really worried," she said.

"I admit I am too," Taylor replied. "It's not like her to miss a meeting."

"Should we report her missing?" Rebecca asked. "She doesn't have any family here that I know of."

"The police usually want to wait 24 hours before filing a missing persons report," Taylor said. "Unless it is a child, there are indications the person is in dire circumstances or has a medical condition. Does Anita have a medical condition?"

"She's never mentioned one," Rebecca said.

"I believe to qualify for a Silver Alert she must be 65 or have some form of dementia, brain disease or injury," Taylor replied.

"Pretty sure that doesn't apply," Rebecca said. "She has so many balls in the air and seems to juggle them all perfectly."

"Tell you what," Taylor said. "Send me a text with her home and work address. I'll call my friend at the SFPD and see what he suggests."

"Okay," Rebecca said. "Thank you. At least we aren't sitting on our hands."

"Try not to worry," Taylor said. "She probably had car trouble or something perfectly normal that kept her from getting here. And you know New Mexico; you can't get a cell signal everywhere."

But Taylor was concerned on the walk back to Piñon Publishing. She hadn't talked with Victor Sanchez in a couple of months. A romantic relationship had seemed possible for awhile but she guessed he wasn't ready. Maybe she wasn't either. Why did relationships have to be so difficult? Taylor felt they were still friends. Nothing bad had happened between them; just the usual work and life that kept everyone busy. She hoped he would be willing to help her.

She entered the Piñon Publishing offices. Inside the vestibule the office had added for security after the former owner had been murdered, she started to depress the call button. Candi, the office receptionist, saw her and buzzed her in. Candi was the only person who could work Mission Control as Taylor called the phone and security system. The entire office would likely fall apart without her.

"Hi Taylor," Candi said cheerfully. "How'd the Wine and Crime meeting go?"

Candi's latest hair color was soft pink and it looked great on her. She delighted in her full name of Candi Kane and often chose clothing and makeup that cultivated a confectioner's image. Last year, she had worn a white coat and chef's hat during the Halloween holiday.

"Not so well," Taylor replied. "The president is missing."

"Anita?" Candi asked. "I hope she's alright."

"So do I," Taylor said thoughtfully as she passed the shelves of books that Piñon had published over the years. Soon, they would need more bookshelves. She thought that a good problem.

She left Candi to her work and went up the stairs to the second floor. Jim's office door was closed or she would have greeted him, but right now she needed to make a call.

Taylor picked up her office landline and hit the programmed number. After several murders connected to the publisher, she'd decided to add it to her one-touch numbers.

"Santa Fe Police," an irritated man answered.

"Hello, uh, may I speak to Det. Sanchez?"

Chapter 3

"May I tell him who is calling?"

"Taylor Browning."

"Be right with you," he said.

Taylor thought the wait was getting long, but it was only a couple of minutes before she heard his familiar voice.

"Taylor!" Victor Sanchez said. "How's book publishing?"

"It's fine, but I'm calling about something else."

"That would have been my guess," Victor said. "How can I help you?"

"I was at the mystery readers group today. You know the Wine and Crime club that meets at the downtown library?" She knew that was unnecessary information but it came out anyway. "Their president didn't show for the meeting and hasn't answered her cell. They're worried about her. Is it too early to file a report?"

"Well, probably," Victor said. "How long has she been missing?"

"Only today, as far as we know. She works at the Pecos National Historical Park. Someone at the meeting called them and was told she'd left some time ago."

"Okay, that's not all that long." Victor was using his reassuring voice. "It's also in San Miguel County so I have no jurisdiction there. I don't know anyone at the Pecos State Police but I do have a colleague at the Las Vegas Police Department in the same county. I'll give him a call and see if he knows anything. They'll have to decide when to file a report.

"Does she have any family?" Victor asked.

"I'm told she doesn't. "Most of her friends are in the Wine and Crime club. She would obviously know people at work too."

"I'll let you know if the Las Vegas police learn anything. And re-member, people have car trouble, traffic issues. It's probably nothing. We've found people who were reported missing drowning their sorrows at a bar. They almost always turn up."

* * *

But the following morning Anita still hadn't contacted anyone or shown up at work. Rebecca was horribly upset as she spoke with Taylor by phone. Taylor could hear sobbing between words.

"What should I do?" she asked.

Taylor related her conversation with Victor the day prior.

"I'll call him again," Taylor said. "Maybe you should call the Pecos po-lice and report her missing. Tell them about her, how conscientious she is, where she works, everything you can think of."

Rebecca agreed.

"It will be comforting to do something, anything," she said.

"Then we have everything in motion we can do at this point," Taylor said. "Let's check in later. I hope she shows up and this will all prove unnecessary."

"Okay," Rebecca signed off.

Taylor returned the headset to the cradle of her office phone. It imme-diately buzzed.

"Taylor," Candi the office receptionist said. "It's the good detective for you. Line three."

"Thank you Candi."

"Hello. Victor?"

"I have news," he said. "Your friend's car was found by hunters along county road 63A outside of Pecos. I'm sorry, but it is suspicious. Her cell and purse were in her car, along with her notes for the meeting yesterday. It's unusual for a woman to leave those items behind."

"And Anita?" Taylor asked, carefully taking notes on her pad.

"No sign of her. The driver's side door was left open and the front-end was in the ditch."

"What could possibly have happened?" Taylor asked.

"She could have walked home, gotten a ride, any number of things, but she hasn't been seen by her neighbors or her employer," Victor summed it up. "The Pecos police are concerned she may have tried to walk through the wilderness area to find help. She may be lost in the woods."

"Lost? Oh no," Taylor gasped.

"There is something else," Victor said carefully not wanting to upset Taylor unnecessarily. "There have been several disappearances in that area."

"Were they found?" Taylor asked dreading the answer because she had a bad feeling.

"No," Victor said. "They have never been found." He quickly added, "That doesn't mean she won't. Both the police in Pecos and Las Vegas are searching. They've called in rescue dogs, people on horseback and a helicopter."

"Thank you Victor," Taylor replied. "It sounds like they're doing everything they can."

She hung up.

How was she going to tell Rebecca?

Taylor began dialing.

Chapter 4

B ut Rebecca already knew. This time she wasn't making any attempts to cover her crying. She was frantic for her friend.

"I called the Pecos police," she gasped. "Like you said." She stopped again to blow her nose. "I'm sorry ... so worried."

"It's okay," Taylor said. "Please don't apologize for caring. We all need friends like you."

"The thought of her all alone in that forest is so distressing," Rebecca added.

Taylor checked herself before she told her about the other disappearances. Rebecca hadn't lived in Santa Fe for long so maybe she didn't know about them. In fact, Taylor hadn't known about them.

After Rebecca said goodbye, Taylor crossed the hall to Jim's office.

Jim was the publisher's art director. Despite being an award-winning artist, he had at one time been relegated to the basement for sins, real or imagined. But when Jessica Endicott inherited the company, she had reinstated him to his present position.

While his downstairs office had been basic, since moving upstairs he'd hung some of his awards on the walls. They included book covers and art work he'd won prizes for while working for Piñon Publishing. Two of his original paintings had been added, one depicting an urban New York City setting and another of a New Mexico landscape. Taylor hadn't been aware Jim was painting again.

Taylor watched Jim for a moment while he completed a call. His brown hair contained a little more silver and it looked good with his blue eyes.

"Taylor. Come in!" He dropped the receiver in its cradle and waved her into his office. "What's up? Sit."

"You're painting again?" Taylor asked. "I haven't seen that lovely landscape. You got the cholla just right. It looks soft and fuzzy, but oh, it isn't."

"I know what you mean," Jim replied. "I've picked a few thorns out of my legs while hiking.

"It seemed time to go back to painting," he continued. "I may even have an opening soon. I've been in touch with a gallery here and they are interested in showing my work."

"That's wonderful. I want an invite."

"*Mais oui, mon chéri.*" In a French accent.

"What's up?" he asked.

"Jim, what can you tell me about county road 63A?"

"You mean near Pecos?" Surprised. "Why would you want to know about that?"

"Because a friend has disappeared on that road."

"Taylor, that's awful. Have the police been contacted?"

"Yes, the police are aware of it," Taylor explained. "They found her purse and cell in her Honda. The car was in the ditch."

"That's similar to one of the other disappearances," Jim said.

"Victor told me about that, but kept the specifics to a minimum."

"A woman by the name of Emma Tresp was traveling to a retreat at the Pecos Benedictine Monastery. This was in 1998. Why she drove past the monastery is anyone's guess. But her car was found abandoned on 63A, that county road you're talking about."

Taylor leaned forward in her seat.

"Now this was a woman with her wits about her," Jim continued. "At 71, she was a world traveler, experienced in finding her way even in new places. But she'd made the trip to the monastery several times before so she was familiar with the area."

"What happened?" Taylor prompted.

"Her car was found about two miles from the abandoned fire tower where the road ends. Rangers once used it for spotting wildfires in the Pecos Wilderness. Her car was wedged against a rock in the road, oil pan damaged but still drivable. The road is dirt and deeply rutted. The farther you drive, the worse it is. There is no way she could have confused this road with the paved one that passes the monastery. She traveled some rough terrain before getting stranded. She had to know she was on the wrong road when she encountered the cattle guard."

"Did they find anything in her car?" Taylor hated to ask.

"Her purse and cell phone were found in the car along with her baggage and belongings," Jim replied. "If she had only walked back toward Pecos, she would have eventually picked up a signal and could have made a call for help. There are a few houses off the road where, at least at night, she could have seen lights.

"And this woman was not found?" Taylor asked.

"No," Jim said. "Hundreds of rescue workers made a concerted effort to find her. They tried everything: teams on foot, horseback and ATVs searched by ground. Helicopters and planes looked for any sign of her from the air. Search dogs never picked up her scent past the vicinity of her car. There was even a hefty reward offered. At the time, $20,000 was a fortune."

"What about an animal?" Taylor asked. "Could she have been attacked?"

"There was no sign of an attack like that," Jim said. "They found her footprints around her car, but none of them led anywhere. It was as if she vanished."

"Geez," Taylor exclaimed. "How can that even happen?"

"There's more," Jim said. "It's been perilous for hunters as well. Melvin Nadel disappeared several miles from the site where Emma vanished. He was in his early 60s and in good shape. He owned a gym and practiced what he preached. In late afternoon, he separated from his two friends. They went deeper into the wilderness and Melvin stayed behind to build a blind. When they returned, he was nowhere to be found. Not only could they not find Melvin, but his weapons were gone too. Considering he was dressed appropriately and an expe- rienced woodsman, his friends assumed he would survive. After all, the lights of Santa Fe were clearly visible. But he never returned nor has his disappearance ever been explained."

"That's awful," Taylor said.

"Another hunter named Stanley Vigil was eventually found dead in the Pecos River. He disappeared east of Pecos but still within the gen- eral area. Both were experienced hunters and wilderness savvy. Those aren't the only unexplained departures. There seem to be pockets within the Santa Fe National Forest that claim lives."

"How do you know about these disappearances?"

"Besides living here for years, we almost published a book from a local man who has studied this," Jim replied. "It was fascinating reading. Old man Endicott didn't think it was classy enough for us so he passed on it. The author has made a fortune on investigating the disappearances from this area and globally. I kept his card so if you'd like to talk with him or read his book, up to you. His theory does make for mesmerizing reading."

Jim fished a card out of his top drawer and pushed it across his desk.

Taylor held the card. The front read: "Edward Mescal, Search and Rescue." The back had his books listed. There were many, all about vanishings.

"Jim, this is unbelievable. And to think, Anita is out there where anything could happen to her."

"There's one more thing," Jim said.

"I don't know if I want to hear it." Taylor was increasingly troubled about Anita.

"Just this," Jim said. "The road, 63A, is sometimes referred to as the Camino del Diablo or the Devil's Road."

Chapter 5

Taylor had to stop for groceries on the way home. That made her arrival at home about 30 minutes later than usual. She waited for the garage door to close completely before entering the kitchen. Cheddar, her most recent addition to her cat family, had once tried to make an escape through the garage. She didn't want a repeat.

She opened the door holding two reusable shopping bags as Santa Fe no longer allowed one-use plastic bags and charged ten cents apiece for paper bags. It was annoying to some, but an effort to encourage citizens to become involved in saving the beautiful countryside they lived in. Many plastic bags dotted the roadside, ruining the fabulous views. Better to look out and see piñon, chamisa and the Sangres.

Extracting the door key from her purse while holding the bags was practically a Houdini operation, but she managed. The locks were new, after the stalking incident. She had to remember to turn the key the opposite way from the original locks. The locksmith recommended a different brand in addition to changing the cylinders as an extra precaution.

That accomplished, Taylor stepped inside the kitchen to a winter wonderland of claw-shredded paper towels. Cheddar was still actively mincing what remained of the roll obviously imitating what his big brother had wrought. She set the bags on the counter where the assault began.

"Oscar!" Taylor raised her voice, but the Abyssinian was nowhere to be seen. Oscar loved reducing rolls of paper to dust piles especially when his dinner was delayed.

The Aby strutted into the kitchen and had the audacity to look surprised. His beautifully sculpted face registered the mess but showed no knowledge of what had transpired. Oscar's clown markings raised gracefully on his forehead as if to say, "What happened?"

"Oscar," Taylor used her mom-cat voice. "We've had discussion after discussion about wasting paper products. I thought we had come to an understanding and you were going straight? Or did you decide to mentor Cheddar in your evil ways?"

The elegant ruddy brown cat blinked, admitting nothing.

"You know," Taylor tried again. "I included cat food in my grocery order. You could be more appreciative." Taylor picked up what was left of the roll of towels with its tufts and puckered paper and placed it in an upper cabinet where it would be inconvenient to use however safe from looting felines.

"That's only good for floors now," she said to Oscar while rummaging in the cabinet for another roll. "Oh great, no more paper towels! I hope you're happy."

Taylor thought he looked awfully pleased with himself, despite giving nothing away.

She admired the breakfast nook Jim wallpapered for her while she was in Arizona attempting to inspire author Crystal Visions to hand over her manuscript. It had been a wonderful surprise when she returned home to find Jim and her two cats napping on the breakfast banco. He had also lit her house with lights and farolitos for Christmas.

Remembering the happy homecoming made her appreciate that Jim could be a sweet guy when he wasn't being inappropriate.

She swept the floor with a broom as more paper scraps floated around the kitchen than were deposited into the dust pan. This would require the vacuum and she didn't want to bother right now. With most of it in a fluffy pile, she poured a glass of red and left the mess for later.

In the living room she collapsed on the sofa. Within seconds, both cats were there with her. Oscar guarded her lap from the orange tabby who cuddled next to her thigh. It made Taylor sad there seemed to be this hierarchal feline tradition. She supposed that Oscar would always be top cat in her little domestic world. Cheddar didn't seem to want to be in charge. Maybe he was okay with ancient feline ways. One thing was certain; he was a loving, gentle guy. Sometimes Taylor thought he could read her mind.

Her house, a fixer, was beginning to look like she had envisioned. The living and dining room hadn't been all that difficult. She had patched some nail holes and cracks with putty and painted it herself. Her father had taught her how to spackle and paint. She was grateful for the skills, loved the process and the results. It was feeling like home. Trouble was, she could never remember where she left the ladder and tools. Sometimes they moved from room to room as though by poltergeist.

Her thoughts were punctuated by her cell ringing. It was Victor.

"Hello Victor."

"Taylor, I have some new information." He was all business.

"Have they found Anita?"

"Sorry, no, but there is something the Las Vegas police are wondering about. Anita had a list of attendees for the meeting in the car. Next to one name, she had written 'NO!' At least, we assume she wrote that. Do you know who Gerald Barker is?"

"The restaurateur? Sure. Everyone knows who he is."

"We're you aware he was scheduled to be at the book club?"

"No, but I wouldn't have known," Taylor said. "But now that you mention it, I didn't see him there."

"Would you have noticed?"

"I think so. I know many of the club members and he would have stuck out like the proverbial sore thumb."

"How do you mean?"

"The members are relaxed. Barker always seems to wear the successful businessman suit. That's who he is. It's also difficult to ignore his good looks. I've seen him in his restaurants and television spots. He's had a lot of news coverage lately because of his use of the Mayan Death Pepper, as he calls it. The public is mad about his chile dishes. The wait for his several restaurants can be hours. I would definitely recognize him."

"With this development in Santa Fe County," Victor continued, "my colleague Det. Matthew Shendo with the Las Vegas Police has placed me in the loop. We've been trying to track down Barker so we can question him and determine if there is a connection to Anita."

"Let me know if I can be of help," Taylor said. "I'm willing to go on the search if it will help."

"Okay," Victor said. "I'll let you know." The line disconnected.

Taylor wasn't satisfied with "I'll let you know." She would talk with Jim. Maybe he'd have an idea.

But first, she turned on the local news. It was the usual politics, murder and deadly road rage incidents, but the next story got her attention.

"Authorities are seeking restaurateur Gerald Barker for questioning in the disappearance of Pecos resident Anita Juárez. We reached out to Barker who was unavailable for comment," the pretty anchor said while a film clip showed Barker at one of his restaurant openings cutting a ribbon. "For more, let's join reporter Angelica Evans live in the field."

"Juárez is president of the Santa Fe Wine and Crime club, a mystery readers group and works at the Pecos National Historical Park," the young reporter said standing in front of the park offices. "Co-workers are despondent as Juárez is well-liked."

The clip ran as the reporter did the voiceover showing the Santa Fe downtown library where the Wine and Crime meetings are held and the Pecos National Park office interior with employees working at their desks.

"Barker has been known to New Mexicans of late as the sole purveyor of the so-called Mayan Death Pepper, a popular ingredient at his restaurants.

"This is Angelica Evans reporting. Back to you in the studio."

"Juárez's car was found abandoned on county road 63A; the site of a number of unexplained disappearances," The anchor wrapped. She paused for her empathic expression.

"And speaking of disappearances, what happened to the sunshine?" She woefully segued to the meteorologist, but her expensive smile never wavered.

"Egad, guys," Taylor moaned. "That was painful."

Both cats looked at her questioningly. Oscar raised his clown marking over his right eye in a very human way. Perhaps her cats wondered at times if they needed to understand what she was saying.

Taylor reached for her phone and called Jim.

"Hello Taylor dear."

Taylor ignored the endearment.

"Did you see the news?"

"Sure did. On what planet do you suppose Anita and Barker could know one another?"

"It does seem unlikely. Although Barker was expected at the book club that day, he wasn't a member," Taylor replied. "None of this makes sense. I can't for the life of me understand what was Anita doing on that county road?"

"You mean the Devil's Road?" Jim teased.

"Jim, I need to do something," Taylor said annoyed. "Look for her, anything."

"Why don't we take a mental health day and explore 63A?" Jim asked.

"Do you think it's safe to do that?"

"There will be law enforcement and searchers looking for her. We likely won't be alone. Besides, I've been there before and I'm still here," Jim said. "Of course, I still have the occasional hallucination; mostly glow-in-the-dark episodes."

"Well, I'm willing to chance it," Taylor replied ignoring his comedic effort. "And this time you don't have to beg me to go."

"See you in the morning. I'll drive my 4 x 4; it's higher off the ground than yours." Her cell went silent.

"Why doesn't anyone say goodbye?" The kitties only stared at her.

* * *

Gerald Barker blinked in a structure full of shadows. He didn't know where he was, but the only window was covered by boards on the outside. The light coming in through the slats hinted that sunset was rapidly approaching. He was fairly certain this would be his second night in this place. There was bottled water and energy bars on a table, a chamber pot with a partial roll of TP and a twin mattress with one blanket and no pillow. He thought there must be something in the water because he felt drowsy. But he needed the fluids so he drank it.

He was abducted, he thought, yesterday morning as he left to make the rounds of his restaurants. They caught him in the garage getting in his car after he opened the door. It had been quick and confusing. Something went over his head; he felt a sharp pain in his arm, followed by being walked to a van parked in his driveway. He knew it was a van because he heard the side door slide into place. But he didn't remember the trip here, what direction they went or being left in this room. No one told him why.

Chapter 6

Taylor's eyes opened to the gloom in her bedroom. She glanced at the clock on the bedside table and it read 3:06 a.m. Her feet moved beneath the covers and found two lumps of fur resting there. But they were not asleep. Each was alert and listening. That troubled her.

Someone stalked her last year – even invaded her house before Christmas. That person touched her cats but didn't harm them. She had been easily awakened since then. Maybe it was time to get an alarm system installed. Pushing the covers back, she got out of bed.

Both cats were attempting to go with her. Oscar jumped to the floor.

"Stay here," she told him, placing him back on the bed. She quietly closed the door after her to keep them from following, but Oscar was already scratching the door.

Walking through the short hall, she passed her office. Empty. As she moved toward the living room she was even more uneasy. Once she stepped into the living room there would be no hiding. The combo room which included the dining area was the largest in the house and it was also the darkest.

Where had she left the ladder? She'd been installing a new cover on the ceiling light earlier. Had she left it in the middle of the dining room? Taylor didn't think so. Since she'd not expected to have to find her way through a dark house, it could be anywhere. Taylor preferred not to trip over it in the dark.

She squinted into the gloom and walked toward the slider in the living room. If she could get the drapes open, she'd have the light of the moon without turning on bright lamps.

Two steps and she heard it; a scraping sound in the kitchen. She paused and listened again. This time it was louder. At that moment, she found the ladder in the living area. It fell with a crash; the screw-driver resting on the top rung slid across the room. Taylor jumped back and stood shaking.

Had someone tried to break in; they would be gone by now. She wouldn't be surprised if the neighbors heard that crash, but certainly a stealthy burglar would have. Taylor didn't want to think about the other types of intruders it could be.

She threw the switch to the overhead. "No point in being stealthy now," she muttered.

Taylor tip-toed into the kitchen. Empty. She took a deep breath and raised one thin blind to check outside. Nothing! Nothing but a chamisa rubbing against the window. She sighed with relief and her heart rate began a downward pace. Fire warnings had been out for days the wind was so high. Taylor scanned the yard and saw no humans or even a coyote on patrol. Nor was a vehicle parked anywhere around, certainly not in her driveway. That scrub had an appointment with her loppers.

After being stalked, she was antsy about being alone. Anita's disap-pearance only reinforced her uneasiness. How could things like that happen to nice people going about their business? Yet, they happened to someone every day.

Taylor picked up the ladder and set it against the wall next to the hallway to the bedrooms. With a sigh, she decided not to fold it, but to leave it open for her next project. It was out of the way and she wouldn't knock it over again. Little did she know what a good idea this would prove to be.

She sat on her bed and ordered motion-activated lights for her house. Some were round and stuck to a surface. The second style was about six inches long and made for stairs, but she had an idea for another use. While at it, she ordered enough batteries to power them all. She wasn't getting caught off guard in the dark again. What the heck, she threw in a lantern too. Santa Fe was known for the occasional blackout. She might as well be prepared.

And she made a mental note to call an alarm company for the house. She hated the idea of it, but maybe it was prudent. She wondered who watched the watchers.

It could wait until tomorrow, after her outing with Jim to Devil's Road.

Chapter 7

The following morning was a bit cloudy, but expected to clear by noon. It promised to be a good day for a missing person's hunt. Taylor fed her cats, separately of course, or risk another shredding episode. Oscar and Cheddar were learning to live together as long as there wasn't too much togetherness. The one place they both wanted was on her bed – at the same time. Cheddar had taken to slipping under the sheets while Oscar slept next to Taylor; her guardian.

She chose hiking boots, jeans and a light-weight jacket as even summer days could be cool especially in the mountains.

A horn honked gently in her driveway. She added her wallet to the inside pocket of her jacket, petted the cats goodbye and left by the front door.

Jim's Jeep Rubicon looked out of place in her drive, but she suspected it would be at home in the rough country terrain. He leaned over and pushed the passenger side door open.

"Top of the morning," Jim said.

"Uh, good morning," Taylor replied as she climbed into the Jeep. "Nearly need a ladder for entry."

"Looks like you're up to it."

Taylor buckled her seatbelt and they were off. To where, she wasn't entirely sure. She'd never been to the Pecos Wilderness before, let alone Devil's Road.

Jim took the interstate. Here the highway cut through the Sangre de Cristos weaving a ribbon of concrete to the east. The mountains were not as imposing along this route as those to the north and south, but Taylor thought it would be beautiful at sunset especially along Glorieta Pass. The trip to Pecos, which usually takes about 35 minutes, was accomplished in less by Jim who floored it. Taylor clutched the door all the way. Instead of going into Pecos, they made a left on what passed as a main street. Soon the street became 63, a county road.

After a short distance and still on a paved road, Jim pulled over.

"That's the monastery," he pointed.

It looked like most buildings in the Santa Fe area, long, low and walled. The mountains rose behind the two-story building with at-tached bell tower. Tall pines dotted the property. It looked like a lovely, restful place. A sign read "Benedictine Monastery." The gate was open. On one side of the gate it read "Peace" and "Paz," Spanish for peace, on the remaining side.

"How long has it been here?" Taylor asked.

"Since the late 1940s," Jim said. "But the area was first settled in the eighth century, long before the Spanish arrived."

Soon they came to a cattle guard and clamored over it.

"Here is where Anita should have realized she was going the wrong way," Jim said.

"The road doesn't look too bad here," Taylor observed. "But it's no longer paved."

"That's what I mean," Jim replied. "If she were on her way to Santa Fe for that meeting, she had to know she needed to turn around and go back towards Pecos. It doesn't make sense."

As Jim drove, the road became increasingly rough. He shifted down for the incline. Taylor held on.

"Geez," Taylor said as she bounced in her seat from the bumpy ground. "Why didn't Anita turn around?"

"We may never know," Jim said.

"Are you saying you don't think she'll be found?"

"I think that's possible," Jim said.

But Taylor wasn't so sure. Jim tended to be a bit pessimistic. She would continue to hope for Anita's safe return.

Eventually they arrived on the search scene. The road was cordoned off with yellow police tape. There was a truck parked behind the tape. Authorities seemed to be using it as a base for their search operations. A team of dogs was being dispatched to the search area after first sniffing what looked like a woman's jacket.

"I don't believe it! She drove a white Honda Civic?" Jim turned to Taylor in question.

"Yes," Taylor said. "I'm certain that's her car – the one in the ditch. Why don't you believe it?"

"Because the other missing woman also drove a white Honda Civic."

Chapter 8

Taylor gasped. "Are you kidding me?"

"I wish I was," Jim said. "Granted it is a different year, but it's the same type car."

"Could be coincidence," Taylor replied. But she had to admit, it was an eerie one.

Jim pulled over and they exited the SUV. Jim immediately approached one of the searchers like he knew him. He did.

"Hey Juan, how are you?" They shook hands across the yellow tape. Taylor stayed at the SUV, but could hear their conversation. Juan looked like he belonged to the wilderness: jeans, flannel shirt, cowboy boots and hat. Taylor thought him more comfortable on a horse than in a car; and likely never visited Santa Fe or any other city unless absolutely necessary. He was exactly who was needed to help find Anita.

"Good, good; and you?" Juan asked.

"Much better than the missing woman. Have you guys found anything?"

"Just what you see here," Juan motioned to the car. "Purse, phone, jacket and meeting materials; all left in the car. Let the dogs check her scent on the jacket and phone. Nothing. They trace her to the ditch and stop. It's like the other lady years ago; seemingly evaporated."

"I see they're out searching both sides of the road," Jim prompted.

"Yes, but it appears she went that way," Juan pointed. "I've been on several of these searches and it's been either we find them dead or we don't find them at all."

"Did you bring your horse?" Jim asked.

"Yeah, that's Paco over there, the bay." Juan said. "Rode him from home."

There were three horses ground-tied, standing obediently. The bay was between two chestnuts. Taylor wondered if they were conversing. Did they know how important their jobs were today?

"Any chance we could get through so I could show Taylor the tower?"

"Not today, man," Juan replied. "No one gets through today. Not until the search has ended."

"That Taylor?" Juan asked.

"Yeah, we're co-workers."

"But you want to be more?" Juan asked.

"She's recently widowed," Jim explained. "We're friends."

Juan nodded.

Taylor turned away surveying the unfamiliar area, pretending not to hear.

The San Miguel County sheriff waved at Juan to join them. At least Taylor assumed he was the sheriff since he wore a star.

"Showtime," Juan said. "Wish us luck. But between us, I fear Camino del Diablo has claimed another one."

"Good luck," Jim said.

Three men mounted the horses and rode off in the direction it was assumed Anita had taken. Taylor silently wished them luck too and fervently hoped that Juan was wrong.

"Shall we return to the office?" Jim asked.

"Yeah," Taylor replied. "I've seen all I can stand today. The Pecos Wilderness has taken on an unnatural presence, one that makes me want to leave quickly."

"Then that's what we do," Jim said in uncharacteristic sensitivity.

"Wait a minute. Do you see how those limbs are broken down on those trees? They're all broken at the same height and hanging downward."

"Yes, but what's that to do with Anita?"

"I don't know yet, but I've seen it before," Jim said.

Taylor was overwhelmed by seeing Anita's car, her things, the search party and the broken limbs that looked so sad. She quickly walked to Jim's SUV and climbed in before he did. She wanted to go.

"I didn't know seeing Anita's car would be so upsetting," Taylor said near tears.

The drive back was quiet. There was no longer any hope or anticipation they would learn today what had happened to Anita. How would the search parties find Anita in 1.5 million acres of wild? Was Anita hurt? Confused? Worse? What started out as probable car trouble had turned into a frightening scenario. The lightness of the Wine and Crime club had come to a full stop. Real mysteries involving people you knew and cared about were something Taylor hadn't expected would be a part of being a mystery editor. She wanted to return to the office and edit the new manuscript they were publishing. Maybe it would it take her mind off Anita's disappearance. But in her heart she knew it wouldn't.

Chapter 9

As soon as Candi buzzed her into the Piñon Publishing offices, she motioned her to come over.

"Two members of the Wine and Crime club are waiting in your office," she whispered like it was top secret.

"Who are they?" Taylor asked.

"Gladys Reyes and John MacTavish."

"Thanks Candi. I'll go talk with them."

Gladys Reyes was a former librarian and widow. She had lived in Santa Fe for decades, moving to the city from New England shortly after she married. Her husband died two years ago and she had thrown herself into several extracurricular activities. An avid reader, she was perfect for the Wine and Crime club and was a previous president.

John MacTavish on the other hand, was a retired FBI agent. Taylor heard he was descended from the Ancient Highland Scottish clan. He was a fan of Highland Park scotch and a pipe smoker – at least at home. Smoking in Santa Fe was prohibited most everywhere. A relative newcomer to Santa Fe, most of his life he'd lived in Washington, DC.

He looked uncomfortable in Taylor's office, sitting very straight. He held his pipe and used his thumb from time to time to pack the tobacco in the bowl. Taylor guessed it was a nervous affectation and he would light it the second he was back in his car. He placed the mouthpiece between his lips and thoughtfully chewed on it. His mustache was clipped neatly and grey hair peeked from beneath his driving cap.

Gladys looked at ease in skinny jeans and a denim jacket, even though she'd never been to Taylor's office. But the worried creases on her forehead gave away her mood. So did her hands being grasped tightly in her lap.

"Hello," Taylor said dragging her office chair around to sit with them. She didn't want the desk between them as this was a meeting she wanted to be as nonthreatening as possible. Anita was their friend too.

"How can I help?"

"We were hoping we could help in finding Anita," John offered. "As you know, I have experience in missing person's investigations. I'm also a bit of a wiz on a computer having taken many FBI classes on the subject.

"Gladys also has research skills from her librarian days," he concluded a bit dismissively. Taylor guessed he didn't have much regard for women's talents.

"I knew Anita better than most in the club," Gladys said, ignoring the slight. "I'm afraid she was mixed up in something, possibly dangerous."

"Do you know what?" Taylor asked, feeling her body tense. A look of disgust crossed John's face. It was brief, but Taylor sensed he didn't like being one-upped by anyone let alone a female and felt Gladys had no right to information he was denied.

"No," Gladys said. "But she was out a lot at night. It was very difficult to get her by phone even during the early evening hours."

"What makes you think what she was doing was dangerous?" Taylor asked.

"Because," Gladys paused. "I'm not sure I should say. She told me in confidence, but she is missing." At this point Gladys fished a tissue out of her jacket and dabbed at her eyes. "I'm sorry."

"Don't be," Taylor leaned forward and covered one of Gladys' hands. "Take your time. And yes, I think it's okay to tell considering the circumstances."

Gladys took a breath and continued.

"She told me one day at lunch she was afraid she'd gotten in over her head. I know what your next question is and I don't know what she was referring to. But at that moment, she couldn't rise above her fear and tell me even though I think she wanted to."

"I was at the location of her disappearance today," Taylor said. "It is isolated countryside, but there were search teams on foot, horseback and in the air. If she's there, they will find her." But even Taylor didn't believe that and she thought probably Gladys didn't either.

"So how do you both want to help?" Taylor changed the subject wanting to keep it as positive as possible.

"As soon as the local yahoos are done with their search," John said peevishly. "I'll go to the site and do my own investigation. I was involved in hundreds of missing person cases in the FBI."

He didn't seem to have much confidence in local law enforcement to find Anita. Taylor had noticed at meetings that John always included a reference to the FBI in most of his conversation. Maybe he was a man for whom retirement wasn't a fit.

"I've already copied all the articles I could find on the Pecos Triangle and the Devil's Road," Gladys said. "I've also found several reference books on these types of vanishings. As you know Santa Fe has a propensity for ghosts and odd, er, departures. Our area is considered a cluster for missing persons particularly in the mountains and wilderness. These clusters exist all over the world, but in the U.S. our area is particularly prone to disappearances.

"I've been looking into the drug trade that goes on in surrounding counties," Gladys continued. "Smuggling is the only thing I can think of that would likely go on under cover of darkness. It's possible someone with the many entertainers who pass through northern New Mexico could be connected."

"Next thing, you'll be blaming the opera singers," John scoffed. Taylor shot him a look.

"It is the right time of year," Gladys replied sarcastically but sweetly. Taylor thought Gladys could take care of herself.

"Okay," Taylor said wanting to wrap the meeting. "You're both working from your strengths. It should be helpful.

"And Gladys," Taylor added. "If you remember anything else about what Anita might have been involved in, please don't hesitate to call me. I'll pass it onto the Santa Fe police."

They rose to leave but Gladys had one more thing to say.

"When Anita told me she might be in over her head, she also mentioned something about the service industry. I don't know what that means or if it had anything to do with her being MIA. But there, I've told you everything."

Chapter 10

After they left, Taylor sat at her desk pretending to edit what was to be Piñon Publishing's next mystery release. They felt lucky to get this author. Edgar A. Perry was already well-known and had been with one of the large New York City publishers. After a visit to Santa Fe, he decided to write a mystery using the locale and had sought out a publisher in New Mexico.

His book, *Murder at the Pueblo* was not only a tight mystery but also emphasized the burdens of the Native peoples in the Southwest, some of whom still had no running water, let alone an internet connection.

Perry had made good money on his previous books. Piñon Publishing didn't have the big bucks he was used to, but did have the connections in New Mexico and beyond to get it into the hands of the right people. Of course, they would also submit ARCs for review at *Publishers Weekly*, *The New York Times*, *Kirkus Reviews* and the *Library Journal*, all standard submissions for reviews on new books. All publishers sought out these reviews to get the word out to bookstores, libraries and readers alike.

Taylor's mind floated from work back to the case of the missing club president. If Anita had been involved in something related to the service industry that could include hotels, restaurants, even transportation. That was a lot to investigate. What, if anything, did the departure of Gerald Barker have to do with Anita? Had he really gone astray or was he hiding? Anita's cryptic notation next the Barker's name on the club attendance list wasn't proof of relationship between them, but Taylor was willing to bet if they had one, it wasn't cordial.

Virginia Compton jarred Taylor out of her rumination by knocking on her open door.

"Got a minute?" Virginia asked.

"Sure," Taylor said. "Come in."

Virginia was Piñon Publishing's senior editor and Taylor's immediate supervisor. Her skill in choosing books that sold and editing them precisely was legendary. Taylor had learned a lot in a short time from Virginia. But the woman could fade into the woodwork or wallpaper. Take your pick. To say her makeup had the light touch would be an overstatement. She only wore some light pink lipstick. Her hair had silvered and she didn't care, but many Santa Fe women rocked their grey hair so the fact that she didn't color wasn't indicative of much. But her clothing choices probably were. Each meticulously tailored suit and her mid-height chunky heels were nondescript. Her favorite colors were beige, tan and taupe. She was the opposite in most every way from the fiery Jessica Endicott, the new owner of the publishing house.

Jessica had inherited the company from her husband after he died mysteriously in his locked office. Her face was a composite of cosmetics and cosmetic surgery; her mode of dress voluptuous topped off with expensive jewelry. Fiery red hair matched her temperament. The staff was always more tranquil when Jessica took one of her frequent business trips.

Today, Virginia was dressed in a neat suit and silk blouse with a carefully tied bow. Taylor thought the color was probably closer to taupe than her other favored colors, but it didn't really bother Taylor. She genuinely liked Virginia.

"Well," Virginia said after sitting down. "I've never had a book author ask me that."

"What's that?" Taylor prompted.

"Edgar Perry called and asked if we offered at kill fee should his book not be published by us."

"What?" Taylor said. "That's usually something only magazine publishers tender."

A kill fee or monetary offering beneath the originally agreed upon payment was offered should publication of the story be canceled; a consolation prize along the lines of something is better-than-nothing. But book publishers didn't routinely offer one.

"Yes. I explained that to him," Virginia sighed. "I also told him his book was in the editing stages with a cover in design. The likelihood of his book not being published? Nil."

"And he said?" Taylor asked.

"Doesn't hurt to ask," Virginia replied. "But you know, it does make me wonder why he would dump his big New York publisher for little ol' us."

"That is curious," Taylor tapped her pen on the top of her desk which always annoyed Virginia, but she never said so.

"Something else odd about him," Virginia continued. "His name."

"How's that?" Taylor asked.

"Something about the name took me back to literature classes in college," Virginia said. "I looked it up. It was the name Edgar Allan Poe used in 1827 when he signed up for the U.S. Army. Of course, we already knew Allan was bestowed upon him by his foster parents, John and Frances Allan. Poe was never adopted by them, but they gave it as his name when he was christened. As I recall, his birth parents were both gone by the time he was three. His father abandoned them and his mother died of TB. Edgar was separated from his siblings and the Allan's raised him."

"Did he specify that it was a pseudonym at his contract signing?" Taylor asked.

"No," Virginia said. "Don't have a clue. I suppose he could have had it legally changed, or it's his real name, however peculiar."

"Who knew there were so many mysterious authors out there," Taylor mused. "They all seem to have something inexplicable about them. Don't know if that's writers in general or if it's contrived. But mysteries are good for us regardless."

"So how is it coming?" Virginia asked. "His book, that is?"

"It's fairly clean," Taylor said. "I may have to edit it backwards because I keep getting caught up in the storyline. But that's a good problem."

"Okay," Virginia smiled slightly. "I'll leave you to it.

"Oh," Virginia turned at the door. "I'm sorry to hear about Anita. She was quite likeable. I hope they find her."

"I do too," Taylor said.

Not being able to concentrate on editing, Taylor pulled up her search engine and typed in the URL from the card Jim had given her.

Taylor found the story of the hunter and two friends Jim had mentioned. The details said they set up camp in the Pecos vicinity in 2009. Search dogs followed his scent for 100 metres and stopped. Nothing had ever been found. No bones; no scraps of clothing. The weapons he carried were gone too.

See wanted to talk to this man who apparently knew some of the secrets of the Pecos Triangle. She dialed the number and left a message.

Chapter 11

It had been a long day and Taylor poured a glass of 7 Moons before collapsing on the sofa with her two cats. Oscar claimed her lap as usual, while Cheddar snuggled next to her thigh. She drank with one hand and petted with the other. Cheddar was nearly grown up. His coat was beautiful with a deep orange circle on each side. His face shape was beginning to resemble a tom instead of a kitten. His nature was quite sweet in juxtaposition to Oscar's less temperate style, although Oscar was quite affectionate with Taylor, regularly head-butting her.

She watched out her slider as the sun began to sink behind the Jemez. The sky put on quite a show this particular evening. Dust? Or just because? Taylor thought Albuquerque was seeing Sandia turn its namesake watermelon pinks and reds. She had witnessed it. Sandia at sunset was beautiful beyond description.

The box she found on her front porch remained unopened on her living room floor. It had to be the lights and batteries she ordered.

"Okay guys," she said. "Time to do something constructive." Cheddar remained napping on the sofa, but Oscar followed her across the room. It wasn't a straight line however; he wandered back and forth, sniffing as he went. Perhaps he was conducting a perimeter check.

The box open, Taylor installed batteries in the lights and set them around the house on the floor where they could light her way subtly at night. No more overhead lights at midnight. Her melatonin levels would surely skyrocket and sleep would come more easily.

With several of the lights left over, she placed them in her most often used kitchen cabinets; first in the cat food cubbyhole. Oscar was fond of midnight snacks. Despite this, the sleek, slender cat never gained an ounce.

"Now Oscar," Taylor said to the wide-eyed Abyssinian. "Even your late night snacks can be done without harsh lighting. His lovely head tilted as though he understood every word. Maybe he did. Taylor gave him a slow blink and he returned it with long lashes. What a sweet boy. Taylor was envious. She had to apply mascara to get that look.

Taylor wrapped her arms around him and held him close. He rewarded her with a robust purr.

"What do you think Oscar? Bath time?"

Oscar knew what bath meant and headed for the master ensuite. Abys were notorious water lovers and he was no exception. As Taylor walked through her bedroom she noticed Cheddar had moved from the sofa to the bed and snuggled between her pillows. Funny, it didn't take cats long to adapt to routine. He knew it was bath time too and that bedtime followed. At that moment, Taylor felt so happy with her little feline family.

She ran water in the tub, added bubble bath.

"In or out?" she asked Oscar. After some deliberation, he decided to stay in the bathroom. Taylor closed the door to keep out drafts.

She sunk into the warm bubbles with a sigh. Oscar leapt onto the side of the tub, made himself comfortable and swatted some of the bubbles. His tail twitched tantalizingly close to the water.

"You're going to fall in," she predicted.

Oscar flipped his tail as if to say no way and hopped to the floor. As Taylor watched with astonishment, he gave a small jump. His front paws landed on top of the door knob. With a little twist of his body, he turned the knob enough the door swung open. He walked through with all the confidence of his royal ancestry.

"Where did you learn that trick?" Taylor shook her head. Oscar never failed to amaze her.

Later, tucked into bed with a cat on each side, Taylor thought her life great. If only Anita was found alive, everything would be perfect.

Chapter 12

Gladys Reyes sat in front of her laptop that evening; her tea long ago had gone cold. She had been researching the area's drug trafficking since she had returned from her meeting with Taylor and John.

It worried her that Anita had mentioned being deeply involved in a difficult situation. She was certain it had nothing to do with opera singers or other entertainers as John had suggested. He could be annoyingly acerbic at times.

New Mexico had the sad distinction of having the highest heroin-caused death rate in the country. But heroin was one of the drugs of choice. Crack cocaine and meth were also plentiful and frequently moved through the beautiful Española Valley north of Santa Fe. It was difficult to believe the charming village of Chimayo was part of the valley and also part of the New Mexico drug culture.

Gladys loved to visit the Santuario de Chimayó and the lovely restaurant down the road, as did many residents and visitors alike. But apparently, from what she was reading, the valley's character changed after nightfall.

A recent news report said that Española, a nearby city to Chimayo, had undergone a sting by a slew of government agencies including the FBI, Narcotics Task Force, the Bureau of Indian Affairs, New Mexico State Police, Santa Fe Police Department and the Española Police Department.

Gladys scanned the names of those arrested. She was about to move on when one name caught her attention: Paul Castillo.

"That's interesting," she said to her black lab Jethro lying at her feet. His liquid brown eyes scoped out his mistress' face in case food was involved but found her occupied in screen time. He went back to napping.

She couldn't help but grasp that Paul Castillo was similar to Pablo Castillo who was a member of the Wine and Crime club. Pablo translated to Paul in English. But it must be someone else. Castillo was a common name in the area. Surely he wouldn't be involved in anything like this. She printed off the story in case it went somewhere.

Looking at the freshly printed pages, she noticed a photo. Someone caught her eye. One of the men in the picture looked familiar. She picked up a magnifying glass and studied it closely. There was no way to be certain, but one of the law enforcement officers looked like John MacTavish. But at the time, he would still have been living in D.C. Must be someone who looked like him. And even if it was John, it was in his capacity as FBI agent.

Pablo was a voracious reader and wrote many of the book reviews the club published and emailed to members every month. One of his strengths was he read Spanish and had written reviews of Spanish language books for those in the club who also enjoyed them, with a sidebar of the review in English. A regular show at the meetings, Gladys had noticed him getting into a heated exchange with a couple of the other members on occasion – most frequently with John MacTavish. She didn't know the context, but assumed it was a disagreement over a book or one of his reviews. Nothing worse had developed. He'd always been pleasant to her and Rebecca, the club vice-president.

But the discovery bothered her. Maybe she'd drop over and see if Pablo could confirm the story was about him. She didn't know if she had the gumption to ask him straight out. Gladys looked up his address. Before leaving, she texted the news story to Taylor and John. It might be helpful to them.

"I'll be back in a bit," she said to the lab, patting him gently on the head. Jethro's tail wagged in appreciation. "You're such a good dog."

Jethro quickly raised his head when he heard her car drive away. He ran to the window and looked out. His tail stopped wagging as he moved on point, eyes watching the car's taillights disappear. When they were gone he paced back and forth in front of the window, whining as if he knew something was not right.

* * *

As Gladys approached Castillo's street, she came to a stop sign in the residential area. It wasn't one of the Santa Fe's more affluent areas and she was a little anxious driving there at night. Before she could make the turn a big black SUV blocked her.

"Oh why did I come here tonight?" she murmured.

She tried to move to reverse, but someone got out of the vehicle and approached. Gladys was apprehensive. It was probably someone as lost as she was, looking for directions.

When she saw the familiar face, she relaxed. That was a mistake.

Chapter 13

At work the next day, Candi buzzed Taylor.

"Yes Candi?"

"Det. Sanchez for you on three," she replied.

"Thank you."

"Hello Victor."

"Hi Taylor."

She didn't like the sound of his voice. It was his grim police officer voice.

"Did you know Gladys Reyes?" he asked.

"Did?" Taylor didn't want to hear this.

"I'm afraid so," Victor said. "She was found dead this morning."

"What? Where?"

"Along 63A outside of Pecos."

"The Devil's Road?"

"If you prefer," he said.

"I don't," Taylor was fighting tears.

"What happened?" Taylor asked, not sure she wanted to know.

"Taylor, I'm sorry," Victor said kindly. "It appears she was drugged and left in the ditch. We don't know if the overdose or the exposure killed her. There's nothing to do but wait for the ME's report."

"Dead? I just saw her," Taylor sniffled. "We were trying to help find Anita."

"Who are we?" Victor asked.

"Me, Gladys and John MacTavish. They're both members of the Wine and Crime club.

"She texted me last night." Taylor was trying to absorb what had happened and still be helpful.

"What did she send you?" Victor asked.

"She sent a link for a news story on the drug trafficking in the Española Valley. And said she was going to see a club member who might have been mentioned in the article."

"What club member?" Victor asked.

"Pablo Castillo," Taylor said. "Only in this article it was Paul Castillo. She thought it not him, but wanted to ask if he knew the person arrested."

"Would you please forward me that text?" Victor asked.

"Yes, of course." Taylor sent it to him and returned to the call.

"The other recipient was John MacTavish?" Victor asked.

"Yes, she probably thought sharing it would be helpful," Taylor said. "They were together in my office to talk about it."

"How well do you know Castillo?" Victor asked.

"Not well," Taylor said. "He's another member I know only by name. I did notice he usually sat near the back, a bit away from the others. But I do a lot of public speaking at various groups for Piñon Publishing. There are always a couple of people who do that. Maybe so they can sneak out if the presentation is boring."

"What do you know about this John MacTavish?" Victor asked. Taylor could hear him punching a keyboard in the background.

"Former FBI, Scottish, smokes a pipe," Taylor replied. "He was a bit condescending to Gladys at our meeting yesterday, but nothing threatening."

"This is for your ears only," Victor said. "Castillo has a police record. It is drug related. I'll check in with probation and see if he's still assigned to an officer."

"Can you get a meeting together with the Wine and Crime group tomorrow? I'd like to caution the members. After that, it might be a good idea to suspend the club until we get this case solved. Would 2:00 p.m. work for you?"

"Yes," Taylor said. "I'll get on it."

"Thanks. See you tomorrow." The line went dead.

Taylor immediately called Rebecca.

"Hello," Rebecca answered.

"Rebecca? It's Taylor. I'm afraid I have bad news."

"Has Anita?"

"No," Taylor replied. "It's Gladys."

"Gladys. What about Gladys?" Rebecca asked.

"She's dead," Taylor said softly

"Oh no. What happened?" Her voice broke; clearly distressed by the news.

"She was found this morning in a ditch near Pecos," Taylor explained. "The police believe it was murder."

"Murder!" Rebecca burst out crying. "What is going on?"

"I wish I knew," Taylor said almost as emotional.

"A detective with the Santa Fe Police wants to talk with the club tomorrow at 2:00 p.m.," Taylor said. "Could you set that up at the library?"

"Of course," Rebecca said sniffing. "I don't understand."

"I don't either," Taylor replied. "It may have something to do with Anita's disappearance, but we don't know for sure."

"Okay," Rebecca said. "I'll send out an email blast to the members."

Taylor could hear her weeping as she disconnected.

Chapter 14

The following evening, Taylor joined the Wine and Crime club in the library meeting room. There was no wine or tea. It was a hushed group of people. Many already knew that Gladys was dead. They all awaited any new information the police might have. Rebecca introduced Victor and quickly let him have the floor.

"I'm very sorry for the loss of your friend Gladys," Victor began using her name to make it more personal. "For those of you who don't know, Gladys was found near Pecos yesterday." He was careful not to use the word "body" or identify the road.

"I'm here," Victor continued, "to assure you the Pecos police and San Miguel County sheriff's office has every available officer looking for her killer. While she was found in the Pecos area, she may have been killed in Santa Fe County; therefore we are working with the authorities there to determine what happened."

Victor paused. Several of the members were openly crying. Everyone was feeling the shock of the two horrific events in the past few days.

"Since both the disappearance of Anita Juárez and the death of Gladys Reyes happened to people who are members of this group, I have a couple of suggestions," Victor continued. "I believe this would be a good time to take a break from gathering. I'd like all of you to stay at home as much as possible and keep in touch with one another. Do the fundamental things like locking your doors and taking a look through the peep hole before opening. If you can, go shopping or to appointments with someone."

Murmuring broke out among the group. Their faces wore the look of fear and grief.

One man stood. It was Pablo Castillo.

"You can't make us do this!" Pablo shouted raising his fist.

Oh no, Taylor thought. What is he doing?

"You're correct," Victor said calmly. "And you are?" But Victor already knew his identity. He was testing for cooperation.

"None of your business," Pablo said. "I know my rights, and you can't make us do this. I can take care of myself."

"It's only a suggestion, but it is with your safety in mind," Victor said. "One woman is dead and another is missing. There appears to be a connection to this club. We don't want anyone else to go missing or worse."

"I'm not taking this! I know people. Watch your back!" Pablo yelled angrily as he left the room in a huff, turning over a chair on his way out.

Victor remained quiet for a few seconds; allowing the buzzing to quiet after the outburst.

"Mr. Castillo is correct," he said. "None of you have to do this, but I hope you will until we find the perpetrators."

An arm shot up in the audience. Victor nodded and a young woman stood uncomfortably.

"I live alone," she said. "Maybe I shouldn't have even said that, but what do I do?"

"That's a good question," Victor said. "For those of you who do live alone, if no one is available to go with you, try to make trips to the grocery, worship services, errands during daylight hours. Be aware of your surroundings. Check your rear view and side mirrors before exiting your car. If your car has a camera, place it in reverse to look behind you. Listen for someone walking nearby. Don't be afraid to step away from someone and let them pass. Look them straight in the eye. Carry your cell in your hand. There is a reason many taxi drivers keep their cell in hand. An alternate is to attach your cell to a lanyard and hang it around your neck. If you see something suspicious, call us and get to a place of safety."

"Detective," a man said from the front row. "How long do you think it will take to solve these cases?"

"That's a tough question," Victor said. "We've got two police departments and one sheriff's office involved. By coordinating our information and manpower, we hope to have some answers soon."

Apparently, there were no more questions, but the members of the book club were a sad looking lot.

"Thank you for your time."

Victor joined Rebecca and Taylor who were sitting together.

"Didn't expect that," Rebecca said. "I apologize for Pablo."

"No need," Victor said. "There's nearly always one in these cases who refuses to use good sense."

"Thank you for coming Detective Sanchez," Rebecca said and left to talk with a small group reluctant to leave.

"Is he the one that Gladys found in the article?" Taylor asked.

"We're certain he is," Victor said. "He may have altered his name. But since he threatened an officer, I'll have to talk with him.

"Do you need a lift anywhere?" he asked Taylor.

"No thanks, I'm going back to work. It's only a short walk."

"Okay. That advice is for you too Taylor," he added. "Please watch your back."

"I will." Taylor attempted a smile, but it felt more like a wince.

She watched as Victor approached Castillo who leaned against his car. Victor could take care of himself. Taylor headed back to her office.

Victor called out, "Mr. Castillo. A word please."

Castillo regretted lighting a cigarette. He should have driven away.

"What?" Castillo crossed his arms going for casual, but Victor recognized it as defensive.

"Mr. Castillo," Victor said. "We know you have an arrest record and are on parole. Threatening a police detective isn't a good move on your part."

"I did not threaten you; just told you to watch your back." Castillo tightened his arms and kicked at the curb.

Victor noticed he didn't use a contraction which could mean he was lying. His right hand hovered over his gun. Castillo took note of that.

"Had you stuck around you would have found we agreed on your point."

"Right," Castillo said in disbelief.

"I will file an official report on your behavior," Victor said. "A copy will be forwarded to your parole officer. I'm going to recommend anger management. I suggest you keep a cooler head. Do you understand?"

"Yeah," Castillo said defiantly. He crushed the remains of his cigarette on the sidewalk and got into an older model dark SUV. He carefully looked before pulling out of the space. He didn't want a ticket from an already angry detective.

Victor quickly took a photo of the back of the vehicle with the tag clearly visible.

* * *

When she entered the upper hall at Piñon Publishing, she saw Jim's door open and knocked on it.

"Hey Taylor. Come in."

He saw her face. "What's wrong?"

Taylor sat down in one of his visitor chairs. He came around and sat next to her, grabbing a hand.

"What's happened?" he asked.

"There's been a new development," Taylor said.

"What is it?" Jim asked.

"One of the members of the Wine and Crime club was found dead ... on Devil's Road," she sputtered.

"That's horrible," he said. "Do the police think it's related to Anita's disappearance?"

"They don't know," Taylor said. "The police only hand out bits of information that's been verified. They think she was drugged somewhere else and left along the road." She couldn't bring herself to use the word "dumped." How inconceivable that a human being could be thrown away.

"Would you like for me to pick up food and bring it to your house this evening? I could stay over if you want. I'll stop by my house and leave some food out for Tom."

"You named him?" Taylor asked. "You've had him for months."

"Yeah, I thought the guy deserved a name."

Jim adopted the aging tomcat shortly after Christmas last year. He'd been feeding him on his back porch and one day the guy came up and rubbed his leg. It was all over. Jim picked him up and gave him the indoor life he deserved. Taylor was delighted he had given him a forever home. It was so difficult for animal groups to adopt out older animals. She was proud of Jim for doing it. There was a softy in there somewhere.

"I'd bring him along," Jim said. "But you know cats; it takes a while to warm up to one another."

"It's okay," Taylor replied. "I'd love some dinner, but you don't need to stay over. I'll be fine." But she thought that Anita and Gladys probably assumed the same thing.

"Right now, I've got an appointment with the guy you told me about. I'm going to clear my desk and meet him."

"I hope you get some answers."

Taylor left the office and walked the two blocks to La Fonda. The hotel was located on the southeast corner of the plaza and was often used as a meeting place. Inside the dark expansive lobby it was difficult not to wonder about all the people who had walked these tiles long before her. It was a historical building entrenched at the end of the Old Santa Fe Trail. Although the site has been home to Santa Fe's first inn since the 1600s, it became a Harvey House Hotel in the 1920s when it was designed in what has become known as Santa Fe Style.

As she scanned the reception area she saw a lone man sitting near the fireplace across from the bar.

"Are you Mr. Mescal?" Taylor asked.

"Yes, Edward Mescal. Taylor Browning?"

"One in the same."

He stood and shook her hand. It was a gentle handshake from the hand of someone who had worked with them. His smile was authentic as he motioned her to join him.

Mescal had been exposed to a lot of sun. His jaw was square and strong. A big man, Taylor could see him easily carrying out a person, or a body, from a national forest where he worked. She knew from his website that he was a former park ranger who had retired and joined SAR, the Search and Rescue that was part of the New Mexico State Police.

"Can I get something for you?"

"No thank you," Taylor began. "A friend suggested I contact you. Someone I know has disappeared in the Pecos Wilderness. Thus far, she hasn't been found. I understand you are with the SAR and have experience in the area."

"That's right. If you're talking about the recent disappearance of Anita Juárez, I participated in that search."

"Yes, I am talking about Anita. Can you tell me what happens to people – I understand there are others – who seem to evaporate?"

"We don't know exactly what happens or where they go," Mescal said kindly. "Are you aware of the clusters of missing people?"

Taylor shook her head no.

"A cluster is determined if there are three to 80 people missing in a certain geographical location. There is one in the Santa Fe area. Fifteen people have gone missing in the last decade, mainly the Santa Fe National Forest, but the Pecos area has had several. There are 1.6 million acres so a lot of wilderness to get lost in.

"We think it begins with separation," he continued. "Everything is okay until that person separates from the party they're with or if, in the case of Ms. Juárez, they take a wrong turn while alone in their car or hiking."

"I've heard that some are found," Taylor said. "Why aren't they all found?"

"In about 95% of cases, our canines can't locate a scent past a few feet. It just isn't there," Mescal said. "That hugely limits the chances of finding them. That is the case with Ms. Juárez. The dogs followed hers to the ditch. We think we know what direction she took, but past that, we have no clues."

"But what about air search?"

"We do that too. But it's difficult if someone isn't on the ground actively waving at us with a bright color – like orange. It's hard to see them. So if they are hurt and sheltering under trees or a ledge, we may not get a single glimpse of them.

"Another odd occurrence," he added. "When we do locate them, they may be miles away from the site where they were separated. Sometimes we find clothing or boots in an area that we've already searched.

Oddly, the shoes may have been positioned together like you would store them in a closet and the clothing may be neatly folded."

"You're saying if they are found, they could be unclothed?" Taylor couldn't bring herself to say naked.

"Yes or partially clothed. Sometimes hypothermia can trick the person into thinking they are too warm when in fact, they are cold. Sometimes we find them lying in a mountain stream in the winter. It's disheartening."

"You said they are often miles away from where they were separated. How does that happen?" Taylor asked.

"If we knew that, we might be able to prevent this phenomenon," he said. "How does a person walk nearly 10 miles without shoes? This has happened. We have noticed some commonalities when we do find them."

"Such as?" Taylor was on the edge of her chair.

"People often disappear near a water source. The event may be preceded or followed by a change in weather. And oddly, people are found in the vicinity of boulders or rocky areas. Sometimes the person may be ill or disabled, but only subtly. Obviously if the debilitation was severe, they likely wouldn't be out there at all unless it was a case of a person afflicted with dementia wandering off from a care center."

"You've given me a lot to think about," Taylor said. "Thank you for your time."

"I hope it helps." He stood, but hesitated. "About your friend."

"Yes?" Taylor said hopefully.

"I'm sorry, but I would try to get used to the idea she won't be found."

Chapter 15

Victor greeted the attractive woman, make that gorgeous, who stood on his porch holding a sign.

"Hello Chloe. Do come in."

She set the sign against the house and walked through the door that Victor was holding open.

Chloe Valdez was of French lineage but had kept her married name after her first divorce. Her dress was very Santa Fe. Today she wore a broomstick skirt in black. Her poppy colored "cowboy" shirt was topped with a black vest and she fairly dripped in turquoise jewelry. She was a stunning woman with long black hair, deep brown eyes and cheekbones any model would envy. Her face was expertly made up. Victor tried not to stare.

Chloe and her partner owned the top real estate business in the city, Sun Dancing Realty. Although Victor lived on the less expensive south side near the airport and the police station, Chloe was well-acquainted with all of Santa Fe's real estate including the surrounding towns. The south side was more family-friendly than the historic east-side or the north hills. And it is far friendlier than Wilderness Gate, an exclusive community with gated driveways; inhabited by the rich and famous.

It was Chloe's second visit to Victor's house. Originally, she had done a walk through and evaluation. Victor wanted to think further about selling once he knew the value of the property. She received a call from him yesterday asking her to bring the contract to sell his house.

It had been painful to live there after his wife and daughter's death in a car crash. The other driver had been driving drunk. They were both gone in an instant. He didn't understand why he hadn't moved already. He closed the door to the master bedroom as soon as he'd moved his things into the spare room. His daughter's room was also closed. He'd given away their things, including the furniture. The rooms had been empty since. Some people can live with the ghosts and others can't. Victor set up a make-shift office in the dining room.

"Here's the contract," Chloe said. They both sat down at the dining table Victor hadn't used for eating since the last holiday dinner before the accident.

Chloe went through the contract paragraph by paragraph. When she reached the end, Victor signed it.

"Okay," she said. "That's it. I'll place the sign in the front yard. All you have to do is keep it tidy. In the meantime, I'll look for a condo unit for you."

"Not too far away," he began.

"From the station," Chloe finished his sentence. "Don't worry Victor," she touched his arm. "I'll find the perfect place to begin again."

Victor tried to say thanks, but it came out a mumble.

He watched as Chloe placed the sign into the dry earth between the stones, pushing into the ground with her boot. She got in her car, waved and left.

The sign read, "Sun Dancing Realty," along with Chloe's smiling photo and telephone number. On top a small additional sign read, "Three Bedrooms."

Victor stood by the window a few minutes longer. He traveled in his daydream to an earlier time when he and his wife excitedly moved into the new house. How can dreams go so wrong he wondered? One moment you're a happy family; the next, you don't have a family. His eyes filled with tears. The familiar pain in his chest returned. He would always miss her and expected he would feel this ache for the rest of his life. The price of love is grief, he thought. Angrily, he wiped at his eyes.

His wife had been an avid gardener and she'd made the yard a beautiful place, but the gardens where flowers used to flourish were now choking on weeds. Maybe the new owners would bring them back to life. He hoped so. At any rate, he didn't want to care for a yard now. His sister had been right, he needed to sell the house and move on.

Chapter 16

Candi buzzed Taylor's telephone.

"Hi Candi. What's up?"

"She's back," Candi said. "Be afraid; be very afraid."

"Jessica?"

But Taylor already knew it was her because Jessica burst onto the upper floor yelling for Penny.

"Got to give Alise a heads-up," Candi said speaking of Jessica's secretary who was surely watching her favorite streamer at her desk. Alise didn't have much to do when Jessica was gone but answer the phone. With time on her hands, her nails were impeccable. Virginia gave her manuscript queries to read and return, but she could still be caught staring at her cell.

Her phone disconnected with a click.

Penelope Lane was the somewhat new business manager at Piñon Publishing. Apparently, Jessica had taken an immediate dislike to the New England transplant. Penny had moved at her own expense to Santa Fe to take the job and be independent from her overbearing parents; out of the frying pan and into the fire.

Taylor got up to close her door in time to see Jessica, in a bright purple suit with matching spike heels. Her red hair bounced as she slammed Penny's door behind her. Penny's office was across the hall from Taylor's and adjacent to Jim's office. Jim checked the coast was clear crossed the hall, taking refuge in Taylor's office.

"Oh geez," Jim said, his face grim. "Mind if I escape until this latest kerfuffle is over?"

"Be my guest," Taylor said motioning to a chair. "No one can work while Jessica berates another employee."

"Keep wondering when my turn is due?" Jim said.

"Yeah," Taylor replied rubbing her forehead as a headache threatened.

Across the hall the two women squared off. Penny was petite which usually put her at a disadvantage. Today she was glad she'd bought the boots with heels because she and Jessica were the same height. Penny quietly waited for whatever was about to happen.

"I saw my lawyer," Jessica said.

"And?" Penny said.

"You may not be aware, but New Mexico is an 'employment-at-will' state," Jessica said. "Do you know what that means?"

"Yes," Penny said. "It means an employer can fire an employee for reason or no reason."

"The last time we spoke I fired you, and yet, here you still are," Jessica was becoming more explosive by the moment.

Her voice carried to all of the upstairs offices. Taylor and Jim sat quietly, both sympathetic for Penny. Down the corridor, Virginia looked out her window watching a couple of tourists talk animatedly as they walked down the alley. Virginia gave up editing until peace reigned in the office again. Candi, who was downstairs at her station, removed her headset and crept up the stairs to catch what was going on. She felt no remorse for eavesdropping.

"I told you during that, er, meeting, I will go to the IRS and expose Piñon Publishing's artful accounting procedures if you persist on this path," Penny said. But she wondered what had changed and feared the worst. She hadn't used blackmail before. It looked as if she'd gone too far if Jessica's mood was an indicator.

"As I said," Jessica continued. She was breathing heavily with her newfound information giving her power to get what she wanted. "I've spoken with my lawyer and he tells me I'm not responsible for any negligent or even falsified financial records that any CPA or other employee might do on their own. Not only was the former business manager employed by my late husband, he should have had professional liability insurance to protect him. And I think you know that, right?"

Penny nodded in defeat. She was beaten. Her bluff had given her only a temporary victory. All she could do now was try to get some kind of severance package.

"Don't expect any severance from me," Jessica said as if reading her mind. "I don't appreciate the hired help threatening me. That's exactly what you did. I want you out of here within the hour. Pack up! Virginia will check you take nothing that isn't yours. Understand?"

"You've been quite clear," Penny said, venom dripping from her voice.

Taylor and Jim exchanged looks.

"Good heavens," Taylor said, hand to forehead. "I feel for Penny."

"Me too," Jim replied. "I thought her likeable and it seemed she knew what she was doing."

In Virginia's office, she had already pulled Penny's file and was completing her discharge form. Virginia had seen this before. Jessica was as volatile as her late ex-husband. She thought it must have been a disastrous marriage.

When the form was complete, she called Candi and asked how much Penny was owed. When her hours had been compiled, Virginia hand wrote a check, discreetly added $200 so Penny could at least eat until she secured other employment or returned to the East Coast.

Tiredly, Virginia took the form and paycheck to Penny's office. She knocked on her door.

"Come in," Penny said.

"Penny, I'm sorry," Virginia said. "Here's your final check and I'll need you to sign this."

Penny looked at the check.

"That's more than I'm owed," she said regretfully.

"I'll handle that on my end," Virginia said kindly.

Penny read the form and signed it.

She had already packed her personal photos and wall art into a box, along with some mints and a prescription for Valium.

"Maybe I won't need this anymore," Penny said holding the bottle up.

"I understand," Virginia said. "But this is all I can do." She motioned to the check lying on Penny's desk.

Penny looked about to cry, but was determined not to.

"Do you need to check I'm not stealing trade secrets?" Penny said sarcastically.

"No," Virginia replied. "But I do wish you luck."

"Gee thanks." Penny crammed the check into her purse and picked up the box to go. Realizing she was being harsh to someone who had been kind to her.

"I'm sorry," Penny said. "It's not your fault."

Taylor got up and opened her door. She wanted to say something, even if it was only goodbye.

She and Jim waited in the hall for Penny to leave.

"I'm so sorry," Taylor said. "I wish you the best."

Jim mumbled a quick goodbye and went inside his office, closing the door. He wasn't good at goodbyes – or hellos for that matter.

Taylor watched as Penny walked down the steps, handed Candi her set of keys and left by the front door.

Virginia joined Taylor in the hall.

"What a day," she said. She leaned against the wall; something Taylor had never seen her do. Virginia was always posture perfect.

"Makes me wonder when it's my turn," Taylor said.

"Oh, she's already fired me once." Virginia tried to laugh, but it sounded more like a choke.

Chapter 17

At home, Taylor put her feet on the coffee table, a glass of wine next to her and took a few minutes to do nothing. It had been another bewildering day at the office. While Jessica's deceased ex-husband had not been the easiest person to work for, Jessica wasn't just bad at business, but vindictive as well. She had proved that by serving vengeance cold. Penny probably thought the incident was forgotten and felt safe. But no, Jessica may have been waiting for her moment. Everyone was in the office at the time and could not only be witness to her retribution but it served as a warning too. Taylor had once saved Jessica's life. At the time, Taylor thought she had mellowed, having come close to death. But time seemed to be proving her wrong.

Finding doing nothing unsatisfying, she turned on the TV and waited for the evening news to begin. After the self-important opening that every newscast seems to have, the male anchor read the first story.

"The search continues for well-known restaurateur Gerald Barker," he said. "Barker's whereabouts have been of interest since Wine and Crime president Anita Juárez disappeared on a county road near Pecos. A police spokesperson said that Barker was expected to attend the most recent club meeting. Because Barker is a resident of Santa Fe, the Santa Fe police are conducting a joint investigation with the Pecos police department in San Miguel County where Juárez's car was discovered."

During the story, a photo of Anita was shown in addition to Barker's ribbon-cutting ceremony at his most popular Santa Fe restaurant El Jardín Encantado.

"Barker's fame comes from his popular chile dubbed the Mayan Death Pepper," the anchor continued. "The chile is grown exclusively in Doña Ana County, also known for Hatch chiles."

"In related news," the female anchor took over. "Another member of that Santa Fe mystery readers group has been found dead in the same area where Juárez disappeared. Police aren't saying if the two cases are related."

Video showed Anita's car cordoned off with crime scene tape on 63A where it was discovered and footage of the ditch where Gladys' body was found.

Taylor cringed. How did two people from the Wine and Crime club come to be involved in something so heinous? And then, there was Pablo Castillo who had angrily confronted and threatened Victor. Weren't reading groups supposed to be fun? What was Anita involved in and how did it connect to Barker; or did it?

Her musings were interrupted by her cell phone. It was Rebecca Wilson, vice president of the reading club.

"Hello Rebecca," Taylor said.

"Did you catch the news?" Rebecca asked.

"I did."

"Listen, some of our members still want to get together," Rebecca said. "They want to see if they can solve what appear to be two crimes."

"Oh Rebecca," Taylor said. "I don't know if that's a good idea."

"I agree, but I also understand why they would want to try," Rebecca said. "I've told them they can meet in my garage on Saturday. Would you like to be included?"

Taylor thought a moment, but knew being there would be better than getting information second hand.

"Yes," Taylor said. "What time?"

"At 2:00 p.m."

"Okay, I'll be there," Taylor said and disconnected.

* * *

Gerald Barker woke feeling dizzy and unsure of his situation. He thought it evening but it could be early morning too. What he had dreamed lifted and he couldn't retain it. He felt for his phone but remembered it was gone along with his Rolex. Sitting was difficult. His head felt heavy and he rubbed it gingerly. When he thought he could, he stood up, only to collapse to the floor. Crawling on his hands and knees, he managed the two metres to the table where the water bottle beckoned. He grabbed an energy bar and had dinner – or breakfast?

He tried to clear his head. The last thing he remembered before being kidnapped was adding a meeting to his calendar. He'd planned to attend a reading club, not that he cared about reading anything other than his latest contract or menu additions. He hoped to talk with the woman who ran the club, Anita Juárez. She was one of his supply runners. They were vital to helping solve supply chain issues. He'd been told by his restaurant manager she was making noises about quitting. He had hoped this would be a less confrontational way of speaking with her. It wasn't that he couldn't find someone else, but according to the manager she had been dependable.

But he didn't make the meeting. Some nut job had apprehended him and abandoned him in this awful place.

The thick dust on the floor where he sat seemed to move around him. He'd been drinking the water again. Perhaps it was a hallucination? As the rat ran over one hand, he shrieked like a girl and climbed to his feet. He swore in anger and despair. How could he get out of this and was he even meant to?

Chapter 18

Much as Taylor hated the idea of returning to the office the day after the blowup, she found herself sitting at her desk. Everything felt off kilter as it always did when Jessica had one of her fits of pique. Of course, she was correct, Penny had threatened her. And Penny should have known better. Anyone who tried to intimidate Jessica did so at their own peril. Taylor hoped Penny had learned a lesson.

"Taylor," Virginia said from her open door. "Do you have a minute?"

"Of course, come in, sit."

"I have an application from another business major," Virginia said. "If she's still available, I'm hoping I can place her in Penny's former position."

"Are you the employment recruiter now too?" Taylor said.

"Normally, that would be the business manager's job. Or even Jessica's responsibility. But I think you know Jessica won't get around to it. She's missing in action today."

"I thought it was awfully quiet," Taylor said, suppressing the urge to be catty.

"Yes," Virginia acknowledged. "I have a woman named Aponi Swiftwater. She recently moved here from Arizona and has a master's in business administration; minor in accounting."

"Sounds good," Taylor said. "You might ask her if she has a tough outer shell."

Virginia almost laughed. But she caught herself.

"I'll give her a call," she said. "I hope she hasn't taken another job."

"Let me know how it goes," Taylor said.

Taylor returned to editing Edgar Perry's *Murder at the Pueblo.* Perry was excellent at interweaving Pueblo Indian culture into his mystery storyline. Maybe he'd be the next Tony Hillerman. That being said, he didn't have the wealth of history with the pueblos that Hillerman had with the Navajo, Hopi and Zuni tribes. He was making the effort to catch up. Taylor, who was also doing fact-checking, could see he had done his homework.

Engrossed in her work, she almost missed seeing the young woman pass her open door. Virginia was introducing herself in the hallway.

"Taylor," Virginia said. "Would you mind joining us?"

"Of course."

"Hi. I'm Taylor Browning. I'm one of the editors here; specializing in mysteries."

"Hello. Aponi Swiftwater," the lovely young woman said. "It's a pleasure."

"Please come in," Virginia motioned to her office.

Once inside Virginia closed the door and asked them to be seated. She picked up the manuscript she'd been working on and moved it aside; nothing on her blotter except Aponi's resume. Virginia wasn't a multitasker. She cleared her throat.

"We've had an unexpected opening for a business manager," she began. "I appreciate that you sent your résumé the old-fashioned way because we're a bit retro around here."

Virginia asked her about her qualifications and experience. From what Taylor knew about the duties of the job, it appeared that Aponi was well-suited, if not overqualified. She liked that Aponi seemed comfortable interviewing, but not too comfortable. There is no way to do a job interview and feel completely at ease.

Virginia was coming to the end of the meeting, but asked a question that surprised her.

"How do you feel about working in an office that can be, er, stressful?"

"Is any office not stressful at times?" Aponi said.

"It's not just deadlines around here," Virginia said. "Our publisher and CEO can be, on occasion; capricious."

Taylor wanted to laugh at Virginia's description of their volatile leader, but quickly scratched her chin a little hard to keep the mirth at bay. That had to be the nicest way to describe Jessica. Naturally, Virginia had come up with it.

"Are you saying," Aponi paused. She too was making an effort to be tactful. "Are you saying the person in charge can be ... difficult?"

"Yes," Virginia said.

"It doesn't happen very often," Taylor added. "But it can be, uh, upsetting."

"I can cope with that," Aponi said.

"In that case," Virginia said. "I'm offering you the job."

"I'll take it," Aponi said beaming. "When do I start?"

"How's Monday?" Virginia said.

"I'll be here."

Chapter 19

On Saturday afternoon, Taylor joined the Wine and Crime club at Rebecca's house on the south side. This area of Santa Fe had lovely houses and they were less expensive than those of the north side. Many didn't have the Santa Fe touches Taylor loved such as Saltillo tile and kiva fireplaces. If Taylor hadn't found a fixer on the east side, there was no way she could have afforded to live there. She was fortunate her husband had left her a life insurance policy when he died – although she'd still rather have him. It did allow for her to live a comfortable lifestyle.

She parked her red classic Mustang down the street. From the number of cars, it looked like most of the group had already assembled. Rebecca met her at the front door.

"Hello Taylor," she said. "So nice you could come; through here to the garage. I've got some fans in case it's too warm. I can always open the doors."

Inside the garage, Rebecca had set up a long table with Parisian bistrot glasses and cups. To one side was a smaller table with box wine, tea and coffee dispensers. In the middle of the table two large bowls chips and salsa. These appetizers were ubiquitous in Santa Fe. People were already double-dipping.

"Okay," Rebecca said. "Let's call this meeting to order."

There were only about two dozen people here from the larger group. Everyone seemed excited with two exceptions: John MacTavish and Pablo Castillo. They both wore expressions of superiority and anger respectively.

"We're meeting here rather than at the library because Det. Sanchez asked us to keep a low profile," Rebecca said. "There's a feeling that we might somehow be helpful in solving the disappearance of Anita and the ... uh, death of Gladys." Rebecca was obviously moved by the losses and even speaking them out loud was difficult.

"Who would like to speak first?" Rebecca asked.

John MacTavish immediately stood.

"As a former FBI agent," he began, and several people groaned having heard this statement many times. "I'm clearly the best person to investigate these crimes."

"John, give it a rest," Pablo said defiantly. "Everyone knows you were in the FBI. You don't have to keep reminding us."

"Anyone with a definitive line of investigation in mind?" Rebecca tried to regain control.

"We could go as a group to the Pecos Wilderness," a man offered.

"Do you have wilderness experience?" John asked. "You know people have disappeared there who were expert outdoorsmen."

"How about something we could do from here?" Rebecca said. "Like research."

"What good would that do?" Pablo interjected heatedly. "The Pecos Triangle has been thoroughly researched and there plenty to read on the subject. I don't know what we could add."

"Mr. Castillo," a woman cautiously said. "What we need is cooperation in a congenial manner."

Pablo was up in a second, shoving his chair aside.

"This is a waste of time," he said. "I'm outta here." He slammed the front door as he left.

"Well, maybe this wasn't a good idea," Rebecca said. "Do we want to continue?"

"I don't see any point," John said. "None of you are experienced investigators, just ordinary Joes looking to dabble in a real-life tragedy."

"Excuse me," one man said. "John, I really don't think that tone is necessary. Everyone is traumatized by what has happened and wants to help. There's no reason to insult everyone."

"All of you who are traumatized should go home and clutch your pearls. Let a veteran investigator handle it," John said. "Nothing more to do here." He left, but more quietly than Pablo before him.

"I'm sorry everyone," Rebecca said. "I guess we should follow the detective's advice and not meet until they find out who did this. Fighting among ourselves is not helpful to anyone."

They adjourned.

Taylor held back a few minutes to talk with Rebecca.

"That didn't go well," Rebecca said.

"No," Taylor agreed. "But a couple of hot heads can stir up trouble fast."

"Thanks for coming," Rebecca said.

"You're welcome," Taylor replied. "Sorry about the outcome."

"Me too," Rebecca added. "I'm afraid the club will never be the same."

Chapter 20

The rest of the weekend was uneventful. Monday morning dawned a rare cloudy day. Santa Fe averaged 300 plus days of sunshine. Taylor loved a sunny day, but tried not to be too resentful of the occasional cloud. New Mexico almost always needed rain, being the most water-challenged state in the U.S.

She chose her SUV in case the rain was forthcoming. The Mustang had been detailed and she didn't want a shower to mess it up.

At the office, Candi buzzed her through the vestibule.

"Good Monday Candi," Taylor said.

"And to you," Candi said. "The new girl is upstairs waiting on her instructions; an eager beaver for this place." Candi winked.

"Thanks," Taylor replied. "She'll learn we all trail in ... except you. Do you live here Candi?"

"Yes, I keep a cot in the back," she said matter-of-factly and answered the phone. "Piñon Publishing. How can I help you?" Pause. "Mrs. Endicott is on a business trip. We expect her back tomorrow. Can someone else help?"

"I guess not," she said. "They hung up."

"What's this?" Taylor noticed a poster taped to the wall of the reception area.

"That's Jim's upcoming gallery opening," Candi replied.

Taylor read it.

Don't miss this amazing party at Spirit Vision Gallery featuring the art and paint exhibition of award-winning artist Jim Wells, and hence be a part of this auspicious occasion. Canyon Road.

The date and time followed. There was a photo of Jim in his home art studio looking every bit the artist. He appeared comfortable sitting on a stool in front of a large easel. In his hand, he held a bundle of paint brushes. All around him were completed canvases and several in progress. Most were New Mexico landscapes. It was obvious he loved his subject matter. Next to him stood a weathered leather wingback chair; Tom, his grey tabby, took up most of the seat. He looked quite smug in his lucky retirement from the outdoors. Taylor was happy for Jim. He needed this.

"Spirit Vision?" Taylor said. "Spirit Vision? Isn't that the gallery that caught fire while two women were inside? Very mysterious. I remember reading about it."

"Yup, that's the one," Candi said. "A reporter and her friend barely escaped with their lives. They were there when fire broke out. No caused was determined. The fire department ruled it suspicious. We'll probably never know."

"See you later, Candi," Taylor said. "I'll see if I can help Aponi get started."

Upstairs, she found the fledgling sitting in a guest chair near Jessica's office.

"Good morning," Aponi said, standing up quickly.

"Good morning," Taylor replied. "Sorry to keep you waiting. Usually Virginia is in when we open. I'm afraid the rest of us are a bit tardy in varying degrees. At least Candi was here to greet you."

"It's okay," she said. "Show me my digs and I'll get started."

Aponi was gorgeous: long raven hair, beautiful face and slender body.

"Right this way." Taylor showed her to the office next to Jim's. Another gallery poster clung to his door.

"The offices are smallish," Taylor said. "But there's room for everything. And we all have a window. Jessica's has a small balcony."

Taylor wrote down the office internet password that Virginia had changed after Penny departed Friday.

"Restrooms are across the hall," Taylor said. "I'm next to them. You know where Virginia is. Alise, Mrs. Endicott's administrative assistant, works at the desk adjacent to her office. Break room is downstairs. Help yourself to tea or coffee. Candi brings in pastries every morning; no charge. Mrs. Endicott pays for them. Conference room is off the lobby. If you need copies, the big copier is on the other side of Jim. Supplies are in the basement."

Taylor cringed a little when she mentioned the basement. The accountant who had been with the company when she came on board had tried to kill her there. She preferred to avoid it if possible. Currently, he was languishing in the state pen.

"You're from Arizona?" Taylor asked.

"Yes," Aponi said. "I grew up in Tucson, but my tribe, the Pima, lived along the Gila and Salt Rivers. We are called the River People."

"Oh, I remember reading something about the Pimas," Taylor said. "They constructed many miles of irrigation systems and developed drought resistant corn."

"That's right," Aponi said.

"We published a number of books here besides mysteries," Taylor said by way of explanation. "Metaphysical and Native American subjects too. I find both fascinating.

"Well, I'll let you get to it," Taylor said. "Call me if you have a question. Our extensions are one-touch on the phone."

"Thanks Taylor," Aponi said. "I'm looking forward to getting to know all of you."

"Okay then," Taylor said awkwardly. And she wondered if Aponi had what it took to endure the administrative outbursts that were sure to come. Time would tell, but for now she really liked her new co-worker.

Chapter 21

The following day when Jessica still hadn't returned, Taylor started to worry. Jessica had a close call once before. Taylor saved her by breaking into her house and setting off the alarm. The police and fire departments had responded and she survived. She hoped there was nothing to her feelings of dread.

Candi picked up on the first ring.

"Have you heard anything from Jessica?" Taylor asked.

"No," Candi said. "She was scheduled to return last night via the Santa Fe Regional. I've got her itinerary and it lists a 6:30 p.m. arrival from LAX. She was being met by that expensive limousine service."

"I know the one," Taylor said. Jessica wouldn't be caught, uh dead, taking a common shuttle, she always went by limo.

"I've called her cell, but no answer," Candi said. "That's not unusual. Jessica has her own set of rules."

"Okay, thanks. Please let me know if you hear from her."

"Will do."

But by the end of the work day, no one had heard from Jessica. Taylor arrived home to find two happy cats waiting in the kitchen for her. Both were so cute looking up at her from the floor. She expected Oscar to push Cheddar out of the way, but the orange tabby was nearly grown and would likely outweigh the Abyssinian in a couple of months. Maybe Oscar realized this.

Taylor petted both and cautiously checked the kitchen for a paper towel snowfall, but apparently the feline forecast had been wrong. Everything looked as she had left it.

"Hey, you two," Taylor said. "I think you're finally getting some maturity. Thank you for leaving the kitchen unscathed."

She quickly got out the canned food and gave each one their portion. Oscar got his first. No need to tempt fate by feeding out of order. Oscar was first cat. And Cheddar was the gentlest of creatures.

Pouring a glass of wine, Taylor settled on the sofa as was her usual after work unwind. She turned on the evening news. There was nothing like a nice glass of wine and the disturbing news of the day at once. It was a confusing cocktail.

The news was more unsettling than usual. The female anchor with her coiffed hair and heavy makeup was saying something that didn't make sense.

"Last night at El Jardín Encantado, the restaurant owned by missing businessman Gerald Barker, was the location of what appears to be a massive food poisoning event."

Video of the restaurant façade with two ambulances showed patrons being helped out and treated by EMTs.

"Some customers were admitted to local hospitals including, the Santa Fe mayor, state representative from Santa Fe's district 48 and Piñon Publishing president and CEO. No word on their condition at deadline."

The male anchor took over.

"Many patrons of the restaurant have complained of chest pain, difficulty breathing and dizziness; not common complaints related to food poisoning," he said. "Tests are being done. And the restaurant has closed pending the outcome."

"What on earth?" Taylor said. "She picked up her phone to call both hospitals, but it rang before she could.

"Hi Taylor," Victor Sanchez said. "Have you seen the news?"

"Yes. Just. What's going on?"

"Wanted to let you know that Mrs. Endicott is doing well," Victor said. "They plan to release her tomorrow."

"Thanks Victor. I'm relieved. We've been trying to reach her. But if it's not food poisoning, what is it?"

"Our lab is working on it," he said. "We should know in a few days, maybe sooner."

"Anything else you can tell me?" Taylor asked.

"Not at this time," he said. "It would only be supposition. As soon as we know, we'll notify the media. The health department is working this too."

"Thank you Victor. I appreciate your call."

"I'll be in touch." The line went dead.

"Again, why does no one say goodbye?" Taylor addressed her cats. They looked at each other as if to say, do we need to know what she is saying?

"Okay then. I'm off to take a bath." Oscar jumped down and ran into her bedroom. When she walked in, he was scooting under the bed.

"What's up with you?" she inquired. Without waiting for an answer, she entered the bathroom to find a virtual paper ski resort. Not only the roll of toilet paper currently in use, but most of the waiting rolls in a basket on top of the tank had been eviscerated. There were small heaps of paper on the floor, in the tub; even in the sink!

"Oscar!" But she knew it was futile. He was ensconced under the bed until it was safe to reappear.

Cheddar rubbed her ankle. Taylor picked him up and held him close to her chin.

"Don't worry guy," she said. "I know who is responsible."

Before she could get the broom, her cell rang.

"Hello Taylor." It was Rebecca.

"Hi. What's up?"

"I received a call from one of our Wine and Crime's younger members. She may have information about Anita, but doesn't want to go to the police. Could we meet with you tomorrow?"

"Of course," Taylor said. "Why is she afraid of the police?"

"Her English isn't proficient," Rebecca said. "Coming to the meetings has helped her learn English. Most everyone has been helpful and kind to her. She may also be undocumented, but I don't know that for certain."

"Santa Fe is a sanctuary city," Taylor said. "I haven't lived here very long, but would that make it safe for her to talk with the police?"

"Honestly, I don't know," Rebecca said. "But at least we could hear her out. And maybe speak for her."

"My Spanish isn't good," Taylor said.

"That's okay," Rebecca said. "Mine is not bad. We can probably get the story."

"Then let's meet tomorrow at my office," Taylor suggested. "Would four o'clock work?"

"Perfect," Rebecca said. "See you there."

Chapter 22

Maria was a small woman from Venezuela. Taylor guessed her to be in her early thirties. She looked terrified. Her hands were clasped tightly in her lap and her eyes darted around the room as if expecting trouble. Settled on the edge of her chair, she appeared ready to run in an instant.

Rebecca introduced them but did not include her last name. Maria stood shyly extending her hand.

"*Buenos tardes*," she said.

"*Bienvenidos*," Taylor responded in Spanish. She knew the word for welcome and she hoped Maria would know she meant it.

According to Rebecca, Maria's family had fled Venezuela because of gangs. They found their way to Santa Fe a couple of months ago. Maria loved reading mysteries so she had joined the Wine and Crime club where she had been warmly accepted. She was learning English by reading mysteries on a reader where she could look up meanings as she read.

"Maria knew Anita as they both spoke fluent Spanish," Rebecca said. "Maria asked me if they had found out what happened to Anita and of course, I had to tell her we still don't know. Then Maria asked if we knew that Anita had been transporting chiles at night. And no, I had no idea."

Rebecca exchanged some Spanish conversation with Maria.

"Maria says Anita had to keep it on the down-low," Rebecca said. "She didn't know why the secrecy, but three nights a week she would take delivery of boxes of chiles in Albuquerque. Drive them to Santa Fe and beyond."

"*La pimiento de la muerte maya*," Maria interjected.

"Yes, the Mayan Death Pepper," Rebecca translated.

"The one Gerald Barker's been talking up?" Taylor asked. "The chile that causes the long lines at his restaurants?"

Rebecca translated to Maria, who nodded her head affirmatively.

"Anita worked for *Señor* Barker?" Taylor asked.

"*No, Señor* José," Maria said.

"I don't know what to make of it," Taylor said. "There are chiles all over New Mexico. Are these so special they have to be moved under cover of darkness?"

"That certainly seems to be part of the mystery," Rebecca said.

Maria said something to Rebecca. Rebecca questioned a word she didn't know and turned to Taylor.

"She said Anita frequently drove chiles north of Santa Fe, using mostly country roads," Rebecca said.

"The Taos area?" Taylor asked.

"Yes, but there were others," Rebecca said.

"Does Barker have restaurants in other cities outside of Santa Fe?" Taylor asked.

"Bet we can find out," Rebecca said.

"Maybe you shouldn't," Taylor said. "Gladys was doing research that ended badly. We don't want to add to the body count."

"Okay," Rebecca said. "I leave it to you, who you share this with.

But Maria would like to stay out of it. She doesn't even want anyone knowing her name."

"Tell her I won't let anyone know," Taylor said. "Maybe we can find another way to relay this. But please tell her this was very important. And thank her for coming forward."

"*Gracias esto fue muy importante,*" Rebecca said.

Maria smiled timidly.

After Maria and Rebecca left, Taylor stopped by Jim's office.

"Feel like a late lunch at Del Charro?" she asked.

"Are you buying?" Jim grinned.

"Sure, I'm feeling generous."

Del Charro restaurant was their favorite place for *après le travail* excursions. It was located in the Inn of the Governors, a popular hotel two blocks from the plaza. Popular with hungry travelers and locals alike, it was known for its renowned burgers and green chile.

They walked because the tourist season was in full swing and parking spaces were a rarity. Most every bench in the plaza was occupied by someone taking a few minutes to rest their feet or phone home. Locals met and stopped to chat before rushing on to their jobs. There were visitors ogling the beautiful craftsmanship spread out on Indian rugs under the *portal* at the Palace of the Governors. Only approved artisans were allowed to sell at the Palace. There were bracelets, necklaces, fired pottery, sand paintings and woven treasures from which to choose. Visitors to the City Different would take home their prizes and tell the history of it as explained to them by the Pueblo artist who made it. Often the pottery told a story through the drawings that decorated it.

Across the street from the Del Charro was the Santa Fe River – when it ran. It was bewildering to strangers who came from places with wide, deep rivers flowing through their cities. The current state of the river was a trickle, but when the summer monsoon began it could become a roaring torrent. The brave or stupid would bring out the canoes and kayaks. It was a dangerous dance avoiding all the bridges, but there was always someone who tried.

They settled in at a window table away from the bar and its multiple screens of sports and news networks. The décor was more western than Santa Fean, but the warm woods and the roaring fireplace made it cozy even if a little loud.

Jim ordered a burger with extra green and Taylor the green chile chicken chowder. A couple of top shelf margaritas would smooth out the day.

"Congrats on your upcoming show," Taylor said. "Are you excited?"

"Yeah," Jim said, although he rarely appeared animated and this was no exception. "I've got a few more paintings to finish. Some might be a bit wet when we hang them." He smiled, amused.

"I can't wait to see your exhibition," Taylor said.

"Well, you'll have to," Jim winked. "It's only a couple of days."

"Guess you heard Jessica got caught up in that food poisoning fiasco at the Barker restaurant," he added. "Never been too fond of him; it's like he owns most of the restaurants in town."

"The police aren't certain it was food poisoning," Taylor said.

"Been talking to Victor again?" Jim shuffled papers trying to look uninterested.

"Yes," Taylor replied. "The symptoms patrons were exhibiting didn't quite spell out food poisoning, but he couldn't say anymore."

"I saw Rebecca and someone I don't know in your office earlier," Jim changed the subject. "More on the mystery reader club?"

"The woman with Rebecca told us she knew Anita. She also said Anita was involved in extracurricular work." Taylor said.

"Doing what?"

"Apparently, she was running chiles from Albuquerque to points north using back roads," Taylor explained.

"That doesn't make any sense," Jim said. "Yes, chiles are king in New Mexico. People joke we even eat them on cereal. I can say I did try it once, but it wasn't as good as cow juice; kind of dry."

"And now, we've got that competition with Colorado for the best chiles," Taylor added.

"Yes," Jim said. "The rivalry is heating up. Their Pueblo chile against our Hatch. Excuse me, but we've got more than 100 years of breeding and growing experience. There is no comparison."

Before Jim went bonkers on the growing chile rift between the two states, Taylor brought the subject back around.

"Maria, or the name she is using, said it was the special chile, the Mayan Death Pepper, that is so popular at Barker's restaurants," Taylor said. "My understanding is it's grown in the Hatch area. They are trucked to ABQ and Anita – and presumably others – would take possession and drive them to his restaurants around north central New Mexico."

"Good ol' Hatch, our own Chile Capital of the World," Jim grinned. "I can almost taste the freshly roasted green.

"Has she gone to the police with this information?" he continued. "You know they haven't found Barker yet. He's been missing for at least as long as Anita."

"Right," Taylor replied. "He was expected at the book club meeting Anita was headed to."

"But what about the woman in your office?"

"Maria isn't a citizen yet and is afraid to talk with the police," Taylor said. "I'm going to call Victor and let him know what she said.

"She told Rebecca and me Anita was getting scared driving at night on those country roads. But she didn't know if there was a direct threat or she was ill at ease doing it."

"Maybe that's what happened," Jim said. "She got scared and lost control of her car. She could have tried to walk back through the woods."

"Do you really believe that?" Taylor asked.

"No," Jim said. "With the history of that area, I don't think she would have left the road had she needed to walk back to Pecos. I'm sure as a local she knew the history of disappearances. But sometimes when you grow up with the stories you don't take them seriously, dismissing them as rumor and folklore.

"Look!" Taylor pointed at one of the mounted screens. "A police spokesman confirms a delay in releasing the cause of customer illnesses at El Jardín Encantado," She read the captions running across the screen.

"I can't remember that ever happening before," Jim said. "Usually they want to get information out quickly to avoid another round of illness."

Taylor read the captions again. "The restaurant has been closed and crime tape indicates police are investigating further."

"That's weird," Jim said. "Either it's food poisoning or it's not. Why wouldn't the health department be doing the analysis?"

"You have to wonder," Taylor said. "First, two people missing. And then, Gladys is found dead. Add the restaurant mystery. If it's all connected, how? I'm determined to find out."

"Whoa, girl," Jim said. "I don't want to come to your rescue again."

"Excuse me," Taylor replied. "I had to practically spell out in sign language, *set off the alarm!* That crazed accountant was insisting I drink poison. And there was the backup gun in case I refused to drink the brew."

"Yeah, but I did drive through a downpour to get to you." Jim feigned hurt.

"Yes, you did," Taylor acquiesced. "I'm very happy to still be here to share a meal with you, or anybody for that matter."

Their drinks arrived. They had both chosen the margarita *caliente*. The tequila was infused with green chiles and mango giving the drink a bit of a kick. There were lots of places in the Southwest where a margarita hit the spot, but Santa Fe had made it an art form.

"Here's to solving the mystery without becoming part of it" Jim raised his glass.

Taylor agreed, but silently she was already thinking about doing a little research on her own.

Chapter 23

Taylor had barely beaten the cats' dinner time. Oscar was waiting for her at the kitchen door. He all but tapped his foot in annoyance. His brows were furrowed in reproach. There was no mistaking his disapproval. He wasn't a fan of near promptness. Close enough didn't exist in his vocabulary. A quick look around the kitchen showed no shredded paper, curtains or hand towels. Hurriedly, she emptied two cans of tasty looking cat food and set the bowls on the floor. Cheddar's bowl was at a respectful distance, honoring the cat laws that had existed long before they had climbed down out of the trees – or walked out of water? Taylor didn't think so.

"There you go guys," she said. "Enjoy."

After brewing a cup of tea, she sat on the sofa and called Victor. She wasn't sure how he would react, but felt he needed to know.

No one was home so she left a message.

* * *

Victor was with the police lab team at El Jardín Encantado.

"This place is a nightmare of fingerprints and hair," Billy, the head lab tech told Victor. "Even found some blood. Probably someone cut themselves in the kitchen, but we're sending in all the forensics."

"Has every room been processed," Victor asked.

"We're working our way back to the coolers," he said. "There's so much to collect and catalog. We started with the dining room and then the kitchen. Right now, it's the storage areas. There are several pantries. The place is very organized."

"Okay," Victor said. "Keep me in the loop."

"You got it."

Victor walked in blue booties through the restaurant's kitchen, done in dazzling white and stainless. Everything was left as it was when people began to fall sick. Knives were askew on cutting boards where the kitchen staff cut up vegetables and meats, each carefully separated to avoid the dreaded cross-contamination. Pasta had swollen into a disgusting mess as it had been left in water. From Victor's observation, it looked as if every health code had been followed.

Inside the ample dining room were standard tables and booths with bancos or benches covered with Southwest cushions. Paintings from local artists were hung from the walls adding color and available for sale. Light from ornate Southwestern scones and chandeliers added warmth. Many looked to be refurbished originals rather than reproductions.

The foyer had impressive heavy doors carved with the Zia sun symbol, identical to the one on every New Mexico state flag. Gerald Barker's designers had crafted a high ceiling made of pine *vigas* and aspen *latillas*. The *vigas* were substantial hand-hewn logs supporting the roof. These were the real thing, not the faux ones. They were structural rather than ornamental. Between the beams were a series of smaller branches cut to fit and running the opposite way; the *latillas*.

This was standard Santa Fe style that had evolved over the centuries. The flooring consisted of Saltillo tiles, super-sized, and sealed beautifully giving them a high shine and making cleanup easier. Barker had paid extra for some with animal imprints, prized for their authenticity. As the tiles dried in the sun, the occasional cat or coyote left their paw prints for posterity.

El Jardín Encantado was located on prime property near Canyon Road. The exterior was the usual brown adobe but upscale. Although the parking lot was the requisite gravel, and therefore the spaces weren't marked, the outside was landscaped in high desert country's finest specimens of chamisa, piñon and large prickly pear cactus. It was rumored the prickly pear pads were harvested for margaritas and as an ingredient in the restaurant's dishes. The entrance greeted customers with large urns of flowers. Currently a vast number of blue trailing petunias poured out of the giant pots. During cold weather they would be replaced by pansies. On each side of the covered walkway, a mix of purple asters and pink cosmos floated ethereally in the breeze. Aspen had been planted in groupings on either side of the front entrance. No expense had been spared in the building and landscaping.

Once outside, Victor pulled his cell from the inside pocket of his jacket. He'd heard the tone a few minutes ago. It was Taylor who had called. He momentarily wondered if it was business or pleasure. It was difficult to tell sometimes. He touched the screen to return her call while walking outside in the gathering dusk. He briefly glanced to the west as a boiling orange sun slid beneath the horizon. The sky then turned pink, orange and indigo.

"Man, the sunsets are beautiful here," he said to himself. No matter how long he'd lived in New Mexico, his love of the sunsets hadn't changed. Just the right recipe of dust, smoke and wind made it a daily event. Since his work called him out a lot during the evening, he could take a few minutes to escape the latest avoidable tragedy by watching the fiery ball sink behind the purple mountains.

"Hello Victor."

"Hi. You called?"

"Yes," Taylor said while watching the same sunset from her deck. "I had a visitor today who had some information about Anita, but there's an issue."

"Issue?"

"She is a young woman who has only been in Santa Fe a couple of months, so she's not documented yet," Taylor explained.

"That can take from 12 to 18 months on average," Victor said. "With delays and politics, even longer; there are so many hoops to jump through. One little mistake on a form can throw a wrench in it. What country is she from?"

"Venezuela."

"Venezuelans usually flee to Columbia or other South American countries," Victor said. "It's to her credit she managed to get this far."

"Can you take the information from me?" Taylor asked. "She is afraid to talk with police."

"I'll have to," Victor said. "It's unlikely I could find her to talk with her. And I don't even blame her. If she changed her mind, I could use her as a confidential informant, but I can likely come by this information by another source during the course of the investigation."

Taylor brought him up to speed regarding Anita's nocturnal activities.

"Maria said Anita was afraid of something," Taylor added. "But she didn't say if Anita had been directly threatened by someone or if she was concerned about doing so much driving at night. It could have been something like wear and tear on her car or personal safety issues."

"Why would anyone be transporting any food products at night?"

Victor said. "A truck driver, maybe, but even they pull into a truck stop to eat and sleep. But individuals? That's strange."

"I agree," Taylor said.

"Anything else?" Victor asked.

"Not that I can think of," Taylor said.

"Okay then," Victor said, vaguely disappointed. He wanted a relationship with Taylor, but both of them had lost their partners to death and each was hesitant to venture further into romantic waters. He understood how she felt, but maybe someday. And then he reminded himself that someday doesn't always arrive as expected.

He went back inside the restaurant.

"Hey Billy," he said. "Might want to move onto the cooler sooner than later.

Chapter 24

Spirit Vision Gallery was located on Canyon Road. No matter the business, Canyon Road was the high-rent district in Santa Fe. Situated in the historic east side, galleries, restaurants and other businesses clung to the narrow one-way paved road. In summer, it was difficult to drive through because of the many visitors wanting to see the famous art scene. Its many shops were of the Pueblo style with Taos Blue doors and windows; blue being the color to ward against evil spirits. Many of the adobe businesses located here were in older buildings with pedigrees. The neighborhood was mature and moneyed.

Big Mexican pottery grabbed the eye with bright red geraniums spilling over the edge. Lilacs bordered the narrow street bursting into purple flowers adding a light fragrance to the art stroll.

Every Christmas Eve the farolito walk drew thousands to strut their stuff while sipping cocoa, cider and beverages on the stronger side. The way was lit with farolitos, candles in paper bags, and luminaries, small bonfires made from upright logs. Dogs and humans alike were decked out in colorful lights and Santa hats. It was a long

Santa Fe tradition and usually shoulder to shoulder human traffic moving as one.

Taylor parked her SUV in a spot several blocks away. It was dark, but there were people milling about so she wasn't concerned. There were tourists exclaiming over the beauty of the area. But like her, some were locals busily going to work and shopping. She followed several into Spirit Vision Gallery.

On the surface, there was no evidence of the mystifying fire that had nearly gutted the building. Its white walls gleamed and were the perfect backdrop to the paintings hanging from them. Heavy *vigas* crossed the ceilings. Squinting, Taylor could see some of them had blackened areas but if you didn't know to look you'd never notice the proof of a previous inferno. Interestingly, there were hearts engraved in the wood trim and small tile hearts embedded in the stucco of the arched doorways.

The new gallery owner, Corazón Spectre, was greeting guests. When it was Taylor's turn, she traded her invitation for a program. Corazón introduced herself and thanked her for attending. The exhibition description was titled "New Mexico: Memories and Motion." It included a bio of Jim and highlighted his successful shows in New York City and beyond. Several of the paintings in the exhibition were depicted in the brochure. At the end, there was a short bio about Corazón stating her name meant "heart" in Spanish. That explained all the hearts Taylor noticed. Spectre was the British spelling of a ghostly apparition. Taylor wondered if it was a pseudonym.

The opening included a raffle and guests were encouraged to stay and win gifts. Each program came with a ticket attached. Numbers would be called to alert the winners.

The gifts were small six-inch paintings, but instead of showing the complete picture, they were close-ups of famous locations around New Mexico. Taylor immediately guessed the first one as an image of the church at Ranchos de Taos made famous by Georgia O'Keeffe.

Past the raffle table, in a corner near the door was a bar. The bartender had wine and margaritas available. She asked for a white wine.

"There you are, ma'am," he said.

Taylor winced. So she had reached the age of being referred to as ma'am? Ouch. She pushed that aside and entered the main gallery.

The room had perhaps a dozen paintings. Jim used several mediums and these were acrylic, gouache and watercolors. She remembered Jim mentioning he'd given up oils for health and safety reasons and only used water-based paints now. His pieces also were made up of "found" items such as gauze, chicken wire and sand that added texture and interest to his works. All his canvases started their life as a work of art with a coat of Carmine Red. He bought it by the can and slapped it on with a house painter's brush.

According to the brochure, Jim had been visiting locations around the state that held special memories. The large painting featured as the centerpiece of Jim's exhibition was hanging from a single wall straight across from where she stood in the foyer. It was of the Rio Grande Gorge Bridge near Taos. The gorge it spanned was very deep. At 650 feet above the river, it was the second highest bridge in the U.S.

Taylor had visited it once and found it difficult to get to the bridge lookouts. The vibration from the cars crossing it was disconcerting and it was a dizzying distance to the bottom of the gorge. Built in the 1960s, the two-lane bridge had narrow sidewalks to each side with no protection from vehicle traffic. However, that didn't stop the many who braved the traffic and vibration to behold the beautiful gorge from the bridge.

Taylor crossed the room and read the wall label:

Jim Wells | Notation 2-12
2022
Acrylic on Canvas
60" x 36"
Price $12,000

Taylor drew in a breath that was audible. Wow! She had forgotten Jim used to have one-man shows in New York City where he'd made a bundle off his paintings. He'd been a celebrity making the art scene and the gossip columns.

Once she got beyond the painting's price, she continued reading. Below that was Jim's and the gallery's website addresses. Taylor hadn't known Jim had a website. He was full of surprises lately. She felt a sense of pride for him, pulling his life together and making art. And here he was with an exhibition on Canyon Road. In Santa Fe, it was the ultimate address.

This piece gave a sense of grandeur the gorge deserved, backed by a glorious sunrise. The rays of light were enhanced by what looked like toothpicks giving it a geometric feel from a distance. Jim had repeated this technique for the trusses that supported the arches. Sand added texture to the craggy walls that formed the gorge. Taylor could appreciate why this canvas had been chosen for the showpiece.

On the other walls, smaller works hung with other places that held special significance for him. She was about to look more closely when she spotted Jim, doing an interview with a local reporter. Taylor entered the alcove where he was answering questions and tried to be inconspicuous in a shadowy corner. The woman was holding a recorder under her notebook and quickly scribbled his remarks.

"Taylor!" Jim said. "I'm so glad to see you. Come over, I'll introduce you."

The woman Jim was speaking with was wearing jeans, a turquoise tee and a black jacket. Her long brunette hair was highlighted with natural silver strands and her lovely face was only lightly made up.

"Hi, I'm Rachel Blackstone," she held out her hand still grasping her pen and Taylor shook it. "How do you do?"

"Very well, thank you. I'm Taylor Browning."

"Rachel is a reporter with High Desert Country Magazine," Jim said. "She was also in this very gallery the night it caught fire."

"I heard about that incident," Taylor said. "Sounds like you were lucky to get out at all."

"We were," Rachel said.

Taylor was dying to know what had happened that night but resisted the urge to ask her.

"Taylor is the mystery editor at Piñon Publishing downtown," Jim said.

"Hey, that's great," Rachel replied. "I've read several of your Ancestral Puebloan books; quite helpful in my work. I'll have to try one of the mysteries."

"Jim," Rachel continued. "That's all I need. And from the looks of the packed gallery, I'd say the showing is a success."

"Very nice to meet you both," Rachel added. She quickly disappeared into the crowd, a deadline to meet.

"How's it going out there?" Jim asked.

"It's wonderful. There must be close to a 100 people here. Hard to tell with all these rooms, but it's crowded."

"Don't forget how attractive an open bar and free hors d'oeuvres can be," Jim said. But his faced glowed with actual happiness. She couldn't help herself, she hugged him.

"I'm thrilled for you," Taylor said.

"Thank you." He was flushed with surprise. "I just hope I sell a few."

"No doubt," Taylor said. "I'll leave you for now and see the rest."

After only a few steps, she saw someone familiar. It was Pablo Castillo, the member of the book club who had been verbally abusive to Victor.

What was he doing there? Before she could stop him and ask, he disappeared into the back of the gallery.

Chapter 25

Taylor looked around. No one seemed to be paying any attention to her. She followed Pablo. The kitchen was small, white and clean. There were appetizers on trays set out on the counter and at least a dozen bottles of unopened wine. A woman was preparing another tray of canapés and hovered over the counter squeezing a topping onto the crackers with a pastry bag. She didn't look up from her work.

Pablo dropped the cork from the bottle of wine he'd opened. It rolled across the stainless steel counter and onto the floor.

"You can't be back here," he said.

"Pablo," Taylor said. "I'm Taylor Browning. I've spoken to the Wine and Crime club a couple of times."

"Oh yeah, the publisher," he said.

"Actually, editor," she corrected.

"You still can't be back here."

"I noticed you were here. I thought maybe as a guest," Taylor said.

"No guest," Pablo said, as he opened another bottle. "With a name like mine, service only."

There was that angry man she had seen at the meeting. And he was probably right. From what she had observed, many with Hispanic names were in service jobs. Santa Fe was an expensive place to live and even though the minimum wage was $12 plus per hour, that wasn't enough in an affluent city. The visitors' brochures went out lauding the three cultures (Pueblo, Spanish and Anglo) that represented the Santa Fe area. But there were tensions and resentment Taylor understood. Not from first-hand experience, but in observations she had made since arriving in Santa Fe. These issues didn't make the full-color brochures.

Jobs for those without an education were mostly found in the service industry. And housing? Most people in service jobs had to commute from Albuquerque, Los Alamos and Las Vegas, New Mexico. Housing costs in Santa Fe were mostly prohibitive. Affordable housing was a pipe dream for those who needed it.

The woman behind Pablo kept working. She probably didn't want to get involved.

"You're from the Wine and Crime club are you not?" Taylor asked.

"I am a member," he said and angrily threw down another cork.

"Would you tell me why you were so upset with the detective at the meeting the other day?"

"Don't have to answer your questions," Pablo said. "Leave."

"But I'd like to understand," Taylor persisted. "You weren't just unhappy with his request. You threatened him. He was concerned for everyone's safety."

Pablo walked toward her carrying the corkscrew. Taylor fought the urge to step back. When he was about three feet away, he stopped. Taylor tried to look unconcerned. She noticed the woman had disappeared through another doorway. She was alone with, at the very least an angry man. But was he a killer? At that moment, Taylor thought it was possible. His grip on the corkscrew was tight. But what reason would he have for murdering Gladys and maybe Anita?

"All my life I've been told what to do," he said. "I take care of myself in my own way." He slapped his fist against his chest.

His eyes were cold, his face rigid with rage. She had made this worse by talking with him.

"I'm sorry," Taylor said. "The club means a lot to the members. I was trying to understand, but I obviously can't. I'm sorry I disturbed you."

It took all her courage – something she wasn't known for – to turn her back and walk away. Would she disappear now too? Had she crossed a line?

Chapter 26

"Det. Sanchez!" one of the lab techs yelled.

He hated when they did that. Couldn't he just walk over and talk to him? But he had to admire his enthusiasm.

"Yes?" Victor asked.

"That last cooler," he replied. "Something's not right." He retraced his steps and waited for the detective. Geez, he thought, what's keeping him. He's the one who authorized the overtime so they could check out the back of the restaurant.

"What is it?" Victor stood at the door of the cooler looking inside. It was empty save some gunny sacks lying on wooden pallets. The concrete floor beneath them contained a drain presumably so the whole room could be hosed down. Mats covered the traffic paths.

"We thought it was an empty cooler," the lab tech said. "But then we noticed this." He held up a blue nugget. "We found three of these under the mats."

Victor held the piece in his gloved hand.

"Looks like crystal meth," he said. "But why would drugs be in a restaurant storage room?"

"You're the detective." The tech disappeared down the hall.

"Smart aleck," Victor mumbled.

The manager of El Jardín Encantado got out of his car. He could see that the police were still going through the building. A man wearing a suit was standing under the *portal* looking westward. Usually detectives wore off the rack clothing, but this guy was shattering his stereotype of police detectives.

"Sorry," Victor said as the man stepped onto the walk. "No one allowed in right now."

"José Mendez," The tall man said reaching out his hand. "I'm the manager."

"Hello," Victor said shaking his hand. "Still can't let you in."

"Wanted to know when we might reopen?" Mendez said.

"That depends on how the investigation goes. Right now, we're still collecting evidence."

"I can't believe that our patrons could have gotten food poisoning," Mendez said. "We are meticulous in our food handling."

"That's what we hope the investigation reveals," Victor said. But he was only answering with cop platitudes. He was giving Mendez a good onceover. Tall, tan, white teeth, dressed to the nines. Only the loosened tie was casual. And the car he climbed out of was a black BMW. It looked showroom new. Victor had a good idea what restaurant managers made, and most couldn't afford a luxury car without additional income from somewhere.

"Who orders food and does the inventory here?" Victor asked, casually kicking a small stone off the brick step where he was standing.

"That would be Miguel Velasco," Mendez said.

"Where does he fit into the restaurant hierarchy?"

"Well," Mendez was reluctant to divulge too much. He didn't know what Barker would say if he were standing here. "He answers to chef, plans menus, trains staff and keeps inventory."

"And is he a local boy?" Victor asked.

"Oh no," Mendez said. "He hails from the Basque region in Spain. I believe Bilbao. We were lucky to get him."

"And who is the head chef?" Victor asked. He wished he still smoked. It would make this informal interrogation a bit less threatening. But he'd given it up years ago. Instead, he averted his eyes for a moment to the fading sunset.

"It's Michael Grady," Mendez said. "Hey, what is this? I want to know when we can reopen. Why the third degree?"

"Because the owner has been missing for days, there has been an apparent food poisoning event here and no one is reopening before we know what's what," Victor said in his most authoritative voice.

"Oh Barker's on some spur-of-the-moment trip," Mendez said. "He loves to do that; doesn't tell anyone. Just expects us to pull our weight and his too."

"You're not worried about him?" Victor asked.

"No. Like I said; he takes off."

"And tells no one where he is?" Victor asked. "He owns a string of restaurants in Santa Fe and surrounds. That doesn't sound like good business."

"You cops are all alike. I'm done here." Mendez stormed off across the drive to his car. Victor continued to watch him as he spun some gravel.

"I've heard that before," Victor mumbled to himself as he watched him go.

If by chance some of the meth had gotten into the food that could explain the resulting illnesses of the restaurant patrons. The lab guys would have their hands full with this and the press would have a field day. And now he had three more people of interest.

What was it he'd thought about Santa Fe being a less challenging crime scene than Albuquerque? With Barker still missing, one murder and second missing person, he wondered how far all this would go. How did the book club fit in?

Chapter 27

Jim's opening had been an overwhelming success. Of course, he was reluctant to allow himself to be outwardly happy, but Taylor thought he was. Tomorrow his paintings would be hanging in some of the most tricked out houses in the City Different. Having been a bestselling artist in New York City in a previous life, he would command a handsome price tag. Jim had called it square-inch pricing; the bigger the painting, the more it cost. But galleries usually took 40 to 50 percent of the proceeds. Still, not a bad night's work.

She had stayed through the end and even won one of the raffle prize paintings. Yes, Taylor now owned a Jim Wells original. It was a miniature of the St. Francis Cathedral with the evergreen tree no longer growing there. She was happy to have this particular image and remembered how the tree had stood for nearly a century. The 60-foot spruce, referred to as "Grandpa's tree," by the grandchildren of the man who planted it around 1922, had fallen during the winter in severe winds.

When she returned home, Taylor settled comfortably on the sofa and looked through her sliders at the darkness. It was a soothing thing.

Oscar was on her lap and Cheddar purred contentedly on the arm of the couch in the foo position.

"Do you want to guard me?" Taylor asked the tabby.

Cheddar turned and looked at her with the wise face he was developing and blinked once.

She took that as a yes.

Taylor woke with a start about a half hour later. Cheddar was tapping on her arm. Even when she woke, he continued tapping on her forearm with urgency. He was obviously concerned about something.

"What is it Cheddar?" Taylor asked.

Tabbies are very expressive because of their stripes. The perfect "M" over Cheddar's eyes was drawn together almost making a single line. His golden eyes were wide with what? Fear? He continued to strike softly at her arm with his paw.

Taylor looked at Oscar who was no longer on her lap, but at rigid attention on the floor staring out the slider. His tail swung back and forth fiercely.

Taylor slumped awkwardly. She rubbed her neck while taking a quick survey of the living room.

There it was, a noise that had apparently triggered her cats to deploy full combat mode.

It sounded as if someone or something had hit or lunged against the front door.

"Go hide," she instructed the cats.

Oscar knew what it meant and obediently made tracks to her bedroom. Cheddar followed; a quick study. Her voice must have betrayed her concern. Last year, after the home invasion, she had placed boxes under her bed for them to hide in. With all the other stuff she stored there, they looked like two other cartons. She wasn't the best housekeeper anyway.

She had no intention of opening the door, but carefully stood on her toes to look through the peep hole.

Nothing.

The next noise seemed to come from the kitchen. She crossed the living room again where she quietly closed the bedroom door. The cats would be safe in there; she hoped.

When she walked in front of the wall to the dining room, one of her motion lights came on. She was completely exposed because in her hurry to unwind, she hadn't closed any of her drapes. If the person was looking into her dining room window, he could see her.

"Oh no!" she murmured to herself. She stepped back into the living space and waited for the light to go off. The lights that were supposed to help her navigate her house in the dark were now revealing her location. Had she even locked the kitchen door? She had to find out.

Carefully, she crept along the far wall hoping the light didn't activate. It worked. But she still had to get into the kitchen.

This time it was more like a thud. It sounded as if someone hit the stucco on the outside of her house. If her directional hearing was accurate, it was along the windowless wall. She ran to the kitchen. The light across the room she used to avoid stepping on a cat at night was very bright. Taylor raced across the kitchen and pulled the round light off the wall and slid it into a cabinet, where another light came on. Quickly, she closed the door.

Sitting on the floor in the darkness, she tried to remember where she had put them all. There was another in the short hallway to the garage. She had to get there to check that the Dutch door was locked. Reaching her hand around the corner to check the lock, one of the puck lights came on! Now she was illuminated in the worst possible place. Whoever was out there could look through the kitchen window and see her!

She grabbed the light, pulling it off the wall like the other one. No cabinet to shove it into; she sat on it. Not really comfortable, but all she could do at the moment. Reaching up, she checked both door locks and double checked them. It was secure.

On impulse, she tossed the light onto the banco in the breakfast nook. It might make it look like she was there. It seemed like an eternity but was only about 30 seconds before it went off. That's when the *someone out there* pounded on the back door right where she was sitting. If she hadn't been on the floor very likely she would have hit the wall behind her. As it was, she bent as low as she could and waited, not knowing what she was waiting for, but afraid to move.

Knuckles tapped on the window of the door as if knocking quietly. After all the noise he had made, why be considerate now? Taylor thought she heard footsteps moving away from her house. Was it over?

Slowly, she rose. When she was on her knees, she lifted the blinds that covered the glass in the upper door. There was something attached to the pane, but she would have to get higher to see it. She heard a car driving away, but it could be anyone. Taylor waited, her pulse tried to beat out of her wrist. But as it slowed, her brain kicked in and was throwing up red flags. She'd been frightened, but now was trying to make sense of it. Why would anyone do this to her?

The light in the dining room came on. Was he in the house? She braced herself. The only weapon she had was a little puck light. She'd have to startle him with the light and then throw it at the intruder. But the shadows returned and no one entered the kitchen where she huddled in fearful anticipation.

No one that is, but Oscar, who ambled over to her and butted her leg.

"Are you sounding the all clear?" she spoke softly and patted his angular head with its smooth ruddy fur.

"Say, how did you get out of the bedroom? I must not have closed the door completely." Oscar purred and she felt safer.

"Okay Oscar, the moment of truth."

Taylor stood and warily looked through the blinds. All she could see was a white piece of paper with large black letters made by a printer:

"Stop. Triangle waits!" The triangle was drawn as a symbol.

She gasped.

Never had she closed shades and curtains so fast. It reminded her of a dream she had once. In it, she was trying to cover all the windows in a house. It had many and she could only move in slow motion. She felt that way now even though she was breaking all speed records. When it was done, she returned to the kitchen and snapped a photo of the note taped to her windowpane. She would remove it tomorrow. There was no way she was going outside tonight.

But she had proof of the threat; she texted the image to Victor. A few seconds later, his text showed up.

"Stay inside! I'm on my way. Sending patrol."

She responded with, "Never leaving." Normally, she would have added the scream emoji, but her fingers felt big and stiff.

In a few minutes the officers arrived. One of them identified himself as Officer Rader. He spoke to her through the door.

"We're going to search around your house," he said. "Stay put."

As the two policemen walked away, Taylor overheard one say, "Dispatch said Sanchez called this in?"

"Yeah," Officer Rader said. "She must be someone important."

Taylor was a bit embarrassed, but also glad to see them.

Victor arrived while the officers were still searching. He looked at the note left on her window.

"Don't like that," he said.

"That makes two of us," Taylor replied.

"Cats okay?" Victor asked.

"Yes, we all stayed inside," Taylor said. "Thank you for coming. You didn't need to."

"I was hanging out," Victor lied.

"Can't really imagine that," she said. "More likely fighting crime and arresting the bad guys."

"Guy's got to have a beer now and then." He quickly squeezed her hand to reassure her, but not long enough for the officers to see him do it.

Taylor liked this Victor.

After a few minutes of rustling bushes and moving flashlight beams, the officers returned.

"There's a small dent in the stucco in back," Rader reported to Sanchez through her now open front door. "We also found the note. He gave it to Sanchez already enclosed in an evidence bag."

"File it at the station," Victor told them.

"Yes sir," Rader said.

"Okay, ma'am," he said. "You appear to be secure. Make sure everything is locked. They likely won't come back."

"I have to echo that," Victor said. "Call me if anything else arises."

Likely wasn't all that reassuring to Taylor.

Chapter 28

Back at work, Taylor was startled to hear from Candi that Edgar Perry was live in the office "asking" to see her.

"Are you sure?" Taylor asked.

"Oh yes, Ms. Browning." Candi always called her Ms. Browning when someone was close enough to get an earful.

"Yes, he really wants to speak with you, and I'm about to grab my purse and leave for a meeting." That was Candi's code for a looming all out verbal assault from a guest.

"Please tell him to come up in five minutes," Taylor said. "I need to get Virginia in on this."

"Okay, I'll try," Candi said.

Taylor picked up the phone and buzzed Virginia.

"Help," Taylor said. "Candi's getting her purse."

"I'll be right there," Virginia hung up.

At that moment Edgar Perry burst into her office.

"Now look here," his voice was raised.

Taylor tilted her head as she did when someone was being rude. Geez, you buy their book and lovingly edit and publish it and this is what you get.

He was wearing a colorful vertically striped jacket over everything black. The stripes really did give him a peacock look. Taylor could swear he was wearing eye makeup as his lids appeared lined and a light coating of coal grey shadow finished the look. He reminded her a bit of a fictional character who might appear in a juvenile book. There were two earrings, one a small crescent and the other a long thread of beads. Taylor covered a smirk with her hand and continued to look at him but didn't say anything; a moment later Virginia arrived.

"Mr. Perry," Virginia said in her calmest voice. "Looking all dapper. Would you like to take a seat?" Virginia was doing what Virginia did best; defusing anxious authors. "What brings you to our humble offices?"

"I think you know why I'm here," he sputtered not even trying to be amenable. "I want a kill fee codicil added to my contract. I've heard how publishers treat authors, and it isn't pretty."

"As I explained to you in our prior phone call," Virginia continued as if he was a five-year-old child – certainly the way he was behaving. "A kill fee isn't something that book publishers' offer. That is the realm of magazine or newspaper publishing."

"No one ever told me that," he said smugly.

"Yes, Mr. Perry, I did." Virginia countered.

"But I've read of authors who received a kill fee," he retorted crossing his arms.

"Whatever you may have heard or read," Virginia went on. "We don't offer a kill fee to any author. As long as the manuscript is delivered in full and on time, we publish the book." She smiled pleasantly at him, her hands at her sides. She had avoided forming fists.

Taylor was glad to be behind her desk. She didn't want to be close to Perry. Virginia was holding her own, even leaning forward a little.

"I'm sorry you came all this way for nothing, Mr. Perry," Virginia added. "We are on schedule to publish your book and don't foresee any obstacles."

Virginia nodded at Taylor. Taylor knew what her next move was. She opened her top drawer and removed a card.

"Since you're here, Mr. Perry," Taylor said. "How about having a New Mexican lunch on us? Here's a gift card to The Shed. It's on Palace. Take a left at the intersection and look for their sign hanging under the *portal*." She pushed the card to the edge of her desk.

He swiped it up in his hand and walked angrily to the door where he turned dramatically.

"I could take my book elsewhere, to my regular publisher." He wasn't quite done.

Virginia and Taylor waited. Taylor would let Virginia reply.

"That would be unwise Mr. Perry," Virginia said softly. "Then we would have to get lawyers involved and you know what a long time that would take. Your book wouldn't get published on time or maybe at all."

"That's why I need a kill fee!" he shouted.

Taylor was about to explode. Virginia raised her hand without even looking at Taylor urging her not to engage.

"Mr. Perry," Virginia said. "Do we have to start this conversation all over again?"

His face turned red. Taylor didn't know if he was getting more riled or if he was finally embarrassed.

"You're both ... witchy!" He sniffed and stormed out.

"Was he wearing makeup?" Virginia asked serenely.

"I believe he was," Taylor replied.

Taylor reached for her phone. "Candi, you might want to step into the ladies room."

"Don't have to tell me twice." Dead air.

"At least once he's outside, he can't get back in again," Taylor said. Candi would be conveniently unavailable to open the door.

"Well," Virginia added. "Just another day in the life of a book publisher. I'm glad all our authors aren't like that. What is it about mystery authors?" She smoothed nonexistent wrinkles on her dress.

"Thank you Virginia," Taylor said. "I'm beginning to get the hang of it."

"Always glad to help."

Taylor thought she saw the slightest of smiles as Virginia turned her back, but if so, it was covert.

Downstairs, Candi took a conspiratorial look from the women's restroom. Perry had left the building.

Chapter 29

Gerald Barker was reeling from the drugs in his water bottle. It was worse than usual. He didn't know why he was here or where here was. Someone had to of missed him by now – days ago. His restaurants needed him. The office needed him. What day was it? How long had he been here?

His thoughts were clouding again. He was certain he could find a way out if only they, whoever they were, would stop drugging his water. But he had to drink. In this dry region; hydration was a must. His assumption was he was still in the state but he couldn't know for sure since the trip was a blur.

Exploring his prison, he observed a large window on one side of the room. It was boarded up from the outside. From what he could see through the cracks, he could be in a forest or even someone's back-yard. Certainly, not the Ritz as the floor was covered in dust and an assortment of discarded boxes, clothing and unidentifiable items in different states of disintegration. He was too drugged to investigate further.

* * *

"Is Barker still on ice?" a man bellowed into a burner phone.

"Yeah," another man answered gruffly. "Still giving him water with something extra. Energy bars to eat. He's comfy."

"Okay, but we may be forced to do something more permanent. It's only a matter of time until the cops figure it out."

"Let me know." He disconnected the call.

Chapter 30

The office had settled since Perry burst in, fired off and left in a huff. It had been Taylor's experience most authors had some sort of – artistic fracture – before their book came out. The local ones would make a personal appearance and the others might make an angry call. The introverts would send an email or text that was passive-aggressive in nature. Taylor attributed it to anxiety about their book turning out as to expectations. First, it was the esthetics of the book itself and then later how well it sold.

No one wanted their baby to show up on the back list before its time. Eventually, the publisher would have to remainder unsold books. Remaindering is the process of selling printed books at drastically low prices to clear inventory for new books. Thus, putting them out to pasture is something no author wants to occur. It's a bit of a dirty secret in publishing. There are wholesale bookstores and liquidators that buy trade and cloth books for a $1 or $2; and sell them for $5 up. Any book marked with a felt tip stroke across the top of the pages, is a remaindered book. The concept is similar to marked down clothing at the end of a season.

Feeling restless after the encounter with Perry, Taylor left the manuscript she was working on and took a walk around the upper floor. Virginia was hard at editing. She did it the old-fashioned way with a blue pen and stick notes. Taylor used this approach part of the time, but was good at editing onscreen as well. It worked best with manuscripts in good shape. While Virginia could concentrate for hours, Taylor needed to move from time to time.

Alise Wyatt, Jessica's secretary, was actually working. Normally, she spent undo time putting her mani-pedi skills to work, touching up her makeup or calling her friends. But if she knew Jessica was coming in, she sprang to work. Today she was opening mail and clipping it together for the staff.

"Hi Alise," Taylor said. "What's up with you?"

"Jessica just called," she said. "She will be here in a few minutes."

That explained the sudden effort to be conscientious.

"She's mad," Alise commented.

"How so?" Taylor asked.

"She spoke with Virginia about Edgar Perry's visit." Alise loudly stapled several papers together.

"Why would that bother Jessica?" Taylor asked.

"She doesn't confide in me." Alise shrugged her shoulders. "And speaking of the devil, there she is." Alise hunkered down over the mail.

Taylor turned to see Jessica had reached the top of the stairs and was walking with purpose down the hall; her heels clicking with each step.

"Nothing to do?" she glared at Taylor.

"She came for her mail," Alise said handing several letters to Taylor. "Saved me some steps." Alise winked.

Taylor was grateful. She didn't want to be the next victim of Jessica's fury. She took her mail and departed.

"Alise," Jessica yelled from her office. "Tell Virginia to get in here."

Oh no, Taylor thought. Virginia didn't deserve a verbal thrashing.

Taylor slunk off to her office, leaving the door open a couple inches. Chin in hand; she contemplated the still unsolved mysteries hovering around the city. She wondered if real mysteries were ever remaindered.

"Guess that would be a cold case," she said aloud.

"Say what?" Jim said while poking his head through the small opening of her door.

"Hi Jim," Taylor replied. "Thinking about remainders."

"Shush," he said finger to lips. "We don't want to scare away any authors. That's worse than a sidewalk sale."

"Come in," Taylor said. "Jessica may be on another slash and burn mission."

"Oh no." He slid through the door and sat down out of sight of anyone walking by.

"Who this time?"

"It may be Virginia," Taylor said.

"She can protect herself," Jim said. "She's the one person here who isn't disposable. She may have to listen to some lip, but she stays in the end, or most of us walk too."

"I was also thinking about the baffling disappearances, the book club, the restaurant and how it's all related."

"Don't forget the Mayan Death Pepper," Jim laughed.

"That too," Taylor said. "I can't help but think there are some con-nections somewhere."

"I've got an idea," Jim said. "You remember the reporter at my opening?"

"Yes," Taylor said. "Rachel something?"

"Blackstone. She covers more than arts. Maybe you should talk with her. Rumor has it she's solved some strange mysteries. She might have some knowledge or insights that could help. I know you aren't going to leave this alone so you might as well talk with her."

"How do I reach her?"

"Hang on." Jim hurriedly crossed the hall glancing in the direction of Jessica's office. In a moment he returned.

"Here's her card," Jim pushed it over to her side of the desk.

"High Desert Country Magazine, Senior Editor," she read. "Thanks. I think I will."

* * *

"How did that idiot author get my home number?" Jessica said already at her boiling point which was considerably lower than water. Today's outfit was canary yellow with a purple silk blouse and matching heels. Already worked up, probably a Cat 3 on the Saffir-Simpson Hurricane Wind Scale. No need to tape the windows.

"He left an incomprehensible message on my service," Jessica said. "Really, Virginia, you're going to have to create a code of conduct for the authors. And see they follow them!"

"Can't imagine any other publisher has a code of conduct for their authors," Virginia answered. "Perry was in earlier, but Taylor and I spoke to him and sent him on his way with a restaurant gift card."

"What did he want?" Jessica relaxed some.

"He wanted a kill fee and we explained to him for the second time that book publishers don't do that," Virginia said. "He's experiencing the 'New Book Apprehensions,' or NBA, as Jim calls it." Virginia hoped to lighten up the situation because Jessica was obviously ready to rumble.

"But how did he get my home number?" Jessica said. "Did someone here give it out?"

"Of course not," Virginia said trying not to rise to Jessica's anger. "Actually, Jessica, it's easy these days to get someone's number, thanks to Google and any number of other search engines. I would advise changing it."

"It's unlisted as it is," Jessica said. "Maybe I'll get rid of the landline."

"That might work better," Virginia said. "If the number shows up on any public records, then unlisted or not, it's out there. But keep in mind, eventually your cell will do the same."

"Fine, I'll change the number," Jessica said. "Don't you have something to do?"

Dismissed, Virginia happily hurried back to her office.

Chapter 31

Later that evening, Jim sat in his art studio in front of a partially completed canvas. He had converted one bedroom a few months ago when he'd decided to do art again. Many of the paintings in the recent exhibition were done years ago and had been stacked in his study, but he had added at least two dozen new ones.

The choice to go back into art was hard-won. He had struggled with his drinking for the years after his greatest triumphs on the New York City art scene. Success doesn't always bode well for the person receiving it and he had been young when it found him. He was a high-functioning alcoholic so he could work, but once home, out came the liquor.

One morning he found himself on the floor of his kitchen, glass still in hand, spilled, bottle of scotch in pieces. After heaving himself up, he'd tried to clean up the mess, but his hands wouldn't stop shaking. He drank more to stop his hands and had finally managed to make coffee. That afternoon he went to an AA meeting. It had been a humbling experience, getting up in front of a roomful of strangers and admitting what he had known for many years; he was an alcoholic.

They hooked him up with a sponsor and he'd emptied the rest of his booze down the drain. On the night of his exhibition, he managed to take a pass on everything but Coke. It was not easy, but he was getting there.

Part of painting was going back to a time when he rarely drank before he was tempted by open bars at his New York City exhibitions and the freewheeling lifestyle of an artist in the big city. The mixing of the paint and the act of holding a brush again was healing.

The aging grey tomcat he had rescued and named Tom was on the stool next to him. Jim had fashioned him a three-sided box on top of the stool with a cushion and velvet liner so as to be gentle on his old bones. The cat wanted to be on his lap anytime he was sitting, but there wasn't enough room on his stool, so he invented a cat seat. Now Tom could be a short stretch away for a head scratch.

It hadn't been that way when he rescued Tom. His fur had been matted and infested with every known varmint that took to felines. Jim had called Taylor and gotten a referral to her vet. She'd shaved his belly of mats, treated him for the pests and checked him over thoroughly. Once the freeloaders were gone, Jim had tenderly bathed the cat in his kitchen sink, using gentle feline shampoo. Although braced for a fight, the old guy seemed to know Jim was helping him and stood quietly until the ordeal was over. Once he was dry, he was a whole new cat.

If he remembered his old life on the streets, it seldom showed. Tom took to indoor living. Occasionally, in his sleep, he would wake yowling as though from a bad dream. Once Tom ran several feet before waking and realizing he was safe. Jim was there to reassure him never again would he be a street cat. His paternal instincts surprised Jim, but he didn't tell anyone. There was his reputation to be considered.

"Isn't that right, old man," Jim said as he slid his hand down the tabby's back. A good diet and plenty of pats and the cat looked like a much younger version. He would even play a little, but some of that was while lying down. No Olympic jumping like Oscar, but there was still some kitten in there.

Tom was good for Jim, who now had a reason to get up on weekends. He also inspired him to paint by being his first subject. He'd never painted a pet before, but he wanted something he'd created to remind him how lucky he was to have this cat. Tom's portrait hung in his home office. All he had to do was look up. It was special to him. No one else had seen it, although he might show it to Taylor some day. She understood the bond between human and animal.

He was working on a forest piece for an upcoming showing. He added a tree. The aspen's white-grey bark with black markings was so striking on its own, but he decided it should have a broken branch. As he stroked on the acrylic something he'd once seen on one of those survival shows, he secretly like to watch, came to mind. He dropped his brush in the water jar, wiped his hands with a cloth and dialed Taylor.

She must have been burning the midnight oil too because she answered on the first ring.

"Hello Jim, what's up?"

"I think I know who took Anita," he said.

"Who?" Taylor asked sitting up in bed.

"Bigfoot!"

Chapter 32

"What!" Taylor exclaimed. She'd given up reading for this? "Well sort of," Jim said. "Remember those trees with the broken branches we saw along Devil's Road? They looked like the trees I saw in a Bigfoot survival show."

"Well, I remember them, the branches," Taylor said, wondering what Jim had been smoking. "But I'm having trouble with the Bigfoot reference."

"Wait just a minute," Jim said. "What I'm saying is it could be someone trying to make us think it was Bigfoot or some other creature of the woods. Or it could really be a creature? The rumors and myths of that area run rampant. Some Native peoples believe that *El Viveron* dwells in the Pecos Wilderness and can shape-shift into a colossal-sized snake and other frightening apparitions. The whole area is fabled to attract UFOs. To this day, mysterious lights have appeared and disappeared with no known cause. Occultists were rumored to conduct ceremonies in the area. UFO investigators and ghost hunting researchers have tried in vain to explain any of it.

And still, people continue to disappear," Jim finished.

"Wow," Taylor said. "I knew about the disappearances, but this is fantastical."

Taylor wondered if this fear of serpents originated with the Mesoamerican Quetzalcoatl, or "Feathered Serpent," who was an important god to the ancient people of Mesoamerica and satiated himself by consuming humans. She had read about this scary deity in one of Piñon Publishing's metaphysical books. There was evidence that many Native Americans had originally journeyed to the American Southwest from Central and South America. Some believed their ancestors had made that voyage riding the back of a turtle. Further, they referred to what is now the U.S. as Turtle Island.

She related this to Jim and asked, "Have there been any reports of feathered serpents?"

"Can't say as I've heard that," he said. "But at this point, I wouldn't be surprised by anything people want to report; real or imagined."

"Well, I won't be sleeping tonight," Taylor said.

"Sorry," Jim said. "See you tomorrow. Sweet dreams."

Chapter 33

Taylor settled into editing the following morning. After a couple of hours, she picked up the reporter's card from her desk. Her fingers turned the card over several times as she thought. She wanted to talk to her, but ask her what? The smuggling throughout the Española Valley was apparently a well-known activity. Blackstone was a busy reporter so being concise was something Taylor wanted to do. She picked up her phone and called the number.

"High Desert Country. This is Stella." A woman with a melodic voice answered.

"Uh, hi," Taylor stumbled. "I'm Taylor Browning with Piñon Publishing. I met Ms. Blackstone the other night at an art opening. I was wondering if I could speak with her."

"Sure dear," Stella said. "I'll see if she's available."

Taylor was entertained for a few moments by Indian flute music. Taylor thought it was haunting and lovely. She could envision the ancient mesas and Puebloan ruins. A raven shrieked in the background lending authenticity. Maybe they should update their hold music at the publishing offices.

"Rachel Blackstone," a confident alto voice broke into her thoughts.

"Hi, I'm Taylor Browning," she began. "We met the other night at the art gallery opening."

"Can you be more specific?" Rachel asked. "I've covered several recently. Oh wait, I remember you. It was Jim Wells' exhibition, right?"

"Yes."

"You work at the book publisher?"

"Yes. Thanks for remembering," Taylor said. "We have a bit of a real-life mystery going on and Jim suggested I talk with you."

"How can I help?" Rachel was all business, but cordial. Taylor appreciated that. She didn't like her time wasted either.

"We have a missing person and a murder," Taylor began.

"The book club?" Taylor could hear tapping on a keyboard and assumed that Rachel was using her computer.

"That's correct," Taylor answered. "It may be connected to the drug smuggling in the valley."

"Okay," Rachel said. "I've got about an hour before my next interview. Are you close?"

"Yes. I'll be there in ten minutes."

"Do you know where ..." Rachel began, but Taylor was already racing out of her office.

Taylor made the somewhat exciting turn onto the one-way street to reach the magazine office. The turn was tight off Agua Fria and there was no room for mistakes. The street was short and she could see the building coming up. It was one of the city-approved brown colors. Jim had mentioned there was no sign. John Muir publishing had once been in Santa Fe and they refused to put out a sign, saying "We know where we work." She made another quick turn into the small parking lot and squeezed into the only remaining spot.

The building had once been a single story, but a recent reno had added an upper floor. She walked through the gate into the courtyard where she was delighted to find a small pool complete with fountain. She pushed open the Taos Blue door and entered the reception area.

"You must be Taylor Browning," said a lovely blonde who had to be the most elegant woman she had ever seen. She was dressed in a pink suit that Taylor believed to be vintage Chanel. Even at a resale store, that set her back a couple of Cleveland portraits. Unlike Jessica, this woman was a classic. She was willing to bet no one intimidated her. As Taylor looked around the bullpen, she noticed several reporters were using phones, writing in notebooks and striking computer keys as they worked on deadline. Jeans and tees seemed their uniform of choice.

"Yes, I'm Taylor."

"I'm Stella. I'll buzz Rachel. Can I get you coffee, tea, soda?"

"Oh no, but thank you," Taylor said.

While Taylor waited she thought it must be exciting to be in on things before they hit the news.

Stella stood and walked around her desk.

"Go up the stairs. Hers is the first office." Stella pointed.

"Thank you Stella."

"You're welcome." She went right back to work while a small TV played at low volume. Odd, thought Taylor, but whatever works. It made her think of Alise doing her nails.

Rachel Blackstone was waiting at the top of the stairs. She offered her hand and ushered Taylor into her office. She was dressed in jeans, royal purple tee and a black jacket. Rachel wore a single strand of turquoise and amethyst beads. Her brunette hair hung to her shoulders and curved under at the ends. Soft bangs brushed across her forehead.

Taylor immediately noticed the desk with the Zia sun carved in the front.

"Nice desk," she said.

"Thanks, my editor, Julian Brazos, gave it to me after we remodeled," Rachel said. "Do you know about the Zia symbol?"

"Only that it's on the New Mexico state flag," Taylor said. "I'm still a Santa Fe newbie."

"The Zia tribe who created it considers the symbol to be sacred," Rachel explained. "The symbol was misappropriated and now it's used on all matter of tourism products. The Zia use the sun rays because they represent the four seasons or directions. Four is a sacred number symbolizing the Circle of Life. Some businesses fill in the circle with a character or color. Their Circle of Life must remain open to use the symbol properly. This desk was made years ago and it's beautifully crafted. Julian asked for permission from the tribe to use the desk and donated to a scholarship program for Zia students.

Taylor also noticed the large window behind Rachel with a breathtaking view of Mt. Baldy. Some of the ski runs were visible, but not snow covered. In her office, she had a view of the building next door and the alley. If she worked on her positioning, she could see some of the street activity.

Rachel brought her chair around to the front of the desk and offered the guest chair to Taylor.

"Nice view," Taylor said. "You can watch the seasons."

"Agreed," Rachel said. "Until the remodel, I was downstairs in the wide open spaces. I don't miss the gossip tree." She laughed. Taylor relaxed.

"What can I do for you?" Rachel gave Taylor her full attention. "You said something about the drug traffic in the valley?"

"Yes," Taylor began. "As you already know, the president of the Wine and Crime club that meets at the downtown library is missing. Another member was found dead on a county road."

"The Devil's Road," Rachel interjected.

"You keep up?" Taylor said.

"Part of the job."

"What I want to know," Taylor began. "How bad is the drug running in the Española Valley? The missing book club president was reported to be delivering the popular chile, the Mayan Death Pepper, at night using county roads. Have you heard anything about that?"

"No," Rachel said. "I can't imagine that a food product would be secretly delivered at night, let alone using those back roads. One can easily become lost. Only people who have lived here a long time and used those roads for hunting or wilderness activities would know them well enough to drive in the dark. You never know when they will go from road to deer trail.

"I think it more likely that something else might have been on this nighttime delivery route."

"Are you saying Anita might have been transporting something other than chiles?"

"No. Not without proof," Rachel replied. "I'm also not saying that she knew what she was transporting. But I don't for minute think chiles need to be taken for a ride through the rough country of the Santa Fe National Forest."

"I don't know what to think now," Taylor said.

"I will tell you this," Rachel said. "Every story I've written on the drug traffic in the valley has had Gerald Barker's name come up. He's never been arrested, let alone convicted, but somehow he always seems part of the story. But I can't get anyone to go on the record to confirm that for print. And it's possible he isn't involved. It could be his employees. Or his business is not connected at all. But it does make me wary every time I'm assigned a story covering drug trafficking.

"And there's this," Rachel continued. "I was at the opening of El Jardín Encantado. Barker was showing me around the kitchen area. Near the back they have some storage pantries, actually more like rooms where the food is kept until needed. As we approached, Barker yelled out 'press!' I thought it was so everyone was shipshape and doing their job. You know, when a reporter is around certain impressions are desired. Instead of straightening their aprons the door to the last room was slammed shut. I asked Barker why and all he said was, 'They're still stocking that room.' Since it was a restaurant opening, I didn't push for an answer, but now I wish I had."

"And now he's missing too," Taylor said unnecessarily.

"Yes," Rachel agreed. "If I was following this story, I would be looking square at Barker for my lead.

"As an aside: stay out of the Pecos Triangle. I mean it. Don't go there. It's not safe for several reasons."

"Do you believe that people vanish there? Is it haunted?"

"I *know* people vanish in that wilderness," Rachel said. "They don't all lose their way. As to whether it's haunted, I couldn't say. Wouldn't say is more like it. It's an eerie place and probably possessed by things we don't understand. There's a lot of history there."

"Okay," Taylor said. "Thank you for your time."

"Before you go," Rachel said. "I have something for you."

Rachel opened a drawer and took out a small wooden box with an Art Deco design. She opened it and chose two stones.

"This is black tourmaline," Rachel dropped the stone in Taylor's palm. "It protects from spirits and raised activity such as a haunting. This is selenite. It assists with cleansing and is protective."

Rachel pulled a small crocheted bag from the same box.

"Place the stones in this. You'll notice the bag is breathable so air can circulate. When you get them home, cleanse them and then charge in the sun for several hours or overnight in moonlight. After that, carry them constantly.

"I have my office and my home gridded with these two stones. Even my car has a bag of protective stones. If you would like more, check out Chrysalis and talk with my friend Mari-Lynn Alo. She has a fantastic metaphysical store." Rachel wrote down the address on the back of her card.

Rachel was still a moment as if trying to decide what she should say.

"I fell into this paranormal world by accident. I used a Hopi ritual to return the dead. It was a mistake. The gallery you were at the other night, my friend and I almost died there. Please be careful. Carry these crystals on your person and be respectful of the Native people who came before us. There is much we don't – maybe can't – understand.

"If it's drugs, smugglers deal in permanent fixes. Don't become a loose end or a problem for them."

"Thank you." Taylor looked at the brown bag carefully made in a Southwest color. She slipped the bag inside her purse. "I'll make every effort to avoid that."

Since it was on her way, Taylor drove to the Railroad District to find the metaphysical store, Chrysalis. It was located on a side street near Guadalupe. She explored several of the short streets and found it on her third pass. The sign, a simple shingle, hung next to the open gate. Chrysalis was carved into the wood along with a butterfly. The front had a coyote fence about four feet high in front and at least six feet at the back of the courtyard. Traditional coyote fencing consists of cut spruce latillas, essentially sticks, tied to a steel framework and is commonly found in Santa Fe. Taylor loved the name. Folklore said they were designed to keep the coyotes out.

Taylor walked the pathway of large stones to the *portal*. Before opening the door she enjoyed the colorful courtyard in full bloom with petunias and cosmos. While the cosmos were bright orange and yellow, the petunias complemented them in dark purple. The remainder of the area was done in xeriscaping with indigenous plants of chamisa, sagebrush and piñon. All plantings were designed to use water sparingly. The fish pond acted as a focus for relaxation. Water flowed over stones making a soothing sound. There were chairs placed around perfect for reading and conversation.

The front door invited customers in with a large stained glass work of art. It depicted a Monarch of orange, black and white with a blue background. Taylor pushed the door inward. Several women huddled together in the store's colorful gathering space. They had helped themselves to tea and coffee and were talking excitedly. At times, laughter broke out. The scene made Taylor feel right at home.

A striking woman with waist-length silver hair looked up from the glass case she was stocking. Taylor noticed many women in Santa Fe wore their hair grey with no apologies. She silently hoped her own would look this beautiful – but later rather than sooner please.

The woman's body was draped in soft fabric. It appeared to float around her when she moved. The colors of pale turquoise and lavender made the look sensual, comfortable and a little mysterious.

"I'm Mari-Lynn. How I help you?" the woman asked.

"I spoke with Rachel Blackstone. She told me about your store. Maybe you can help me. Rachel gave me black tourmaline and selenite crystals for protection but I feel I might need something more."

"Do you know what type of protection you need?" She didn't even laugh at her request. In fact, she appeared attentive and serious.

"It may have something to do with the Pecos area," Taylor said. "Have you heard of Devil's Road?"

"Oh yes," Mari-Lynn replied. "The triangle is legend around here with so many disappearances. One doesn't really know what to expect. People claim UFOs are seen there, odd weather events and the Natives tell stories of a large serpent."

"That's what I've heard too," Taylor said. "If I should find myself in that area, what crystal would provide added protection?"

"I would suggest amethyst," Mari-Lynn said. "It's a good overall stone for protection." She placed a translucent light purple stone on the counter.

Taylor picked up the smooth egg-shaped crystal and held it in her hand. It was cool and smooth.

"I recommend to all my ghost investigators to carry peridot. It is believed to protect against evil spirits." She handed Taylor a green stone. "It can calm a spirit to the point it may not upset or harm you."

"That's wonderful, thank you Mari-Lynn." Taylor pulled the knitted bag from her pocket.

"I see Rachel is giving my bags to people who need them," Mari-Lynn said. "That makes me happy."

"You made this?"

"Oh yes. I've made hundreds. If you want more, let me know. I can make them in the different colors for all issues."

Taylor dropped the two crystals in with the others and paid for them.

"Come back," Mari-Lynn said. "And if you venture into the Pecos Triangle, be careful indeed. Make sure you're carrying that bag."

"I will. Thank you."

She placed the bag inside her purse so it would always be close.

On the way back to her office, Taylor mused about what she had learned. If Barker was involved, why was he missing too? Was Anita actually moving drugs rather than food products? Or something else entirely? From what she knew from Maria, Anita didn't know. She made deliveries as instructed. But was she an innocent or part of the some criminal operation?

Chapter 34

José Mendez paced his home office in Wilderness Gate. The Gate was an exclusive living experience southeast of the city proper. Set high enough to look down on the rest of Santa Fe and prized for the night view of twinkling lights of the lesser folks. The five-acre lots pushed close to the Santa Fe National Forest. With a median house price of $3 million, it could go much higher. But with long drives and plenty of gates, privacy was assured for the celebrity owners and others with enough investments to afford elegant solitude.

Mendez picked up his phone and made a call. He was annoyed when it took three rings for an answer.

"Yeah," a man said.

"You keep that phone on you at all times," Mendez voice rose. "I don't wait for you to answer."

"Man, I have to eat once in awhile."

"More likely a beer break," Mendez seethed.

"Whatd'ya want?"

"We need another driver to make deliveries," Mendez said. "I can't keep the $800 HOA fees paid out here without the restaurant open.

Some cop told me the other evening; we won't be opening until they figure out what happened. Cops! Arrogant civil servants."

"Got someone in mind?" the other man asked.

"Yes, and I think we could kill two birds in the process," Mendez said. "Get in touch with this person. I'm sending you a text with the address. Be discreet." He typed a text and sent it.

Chapter 35

Taylor stood at her office window and wished she had a mountain view, but she could see a corner of the plaza park. Some kind of event was being set up. It was difficult to keep up with all that went on in Santa Fe because so many festivals, concerts and arts occurred right in the middle of downtown. She especially enjoyed the weekly summer live music events on Thursday evenings. It was invigorating to listen to the musicians and watch those dancing in front of the bandstand. She now recognized some of the dancers and rooted for them as they twirled and strutted. Some were quite good.

She'd worked a bit of overtime to make up for her appointment with Rachel since it wasn't work related. But now it was time to go before Oscar found some new way to chastise her for lack of promptness.

On her way out, Candi handed her an envelope.

"This came by messenger," Candi said. "Have a good evening."

"Thanks," Taylor said and shoved the thin business-sized envelope in her soft brief case where she stowed manuscripts for later reading.

"You about to wrap it up?" Taylor asked.

"Yes, ma'am," Candi replied. "It's been a day. Is everyone out? If so, I'll set the alarm on my way out."

"I think so," Taylor said. "It was awfully quiet upstairs."

"Just to be sure," Candi winked and turned on the office intercom. "Locking up, anyone left in the building? Last one out is a dangling participle."

"Guess not," Taylor laughed. "See you tomorrow."

In her garage, Taylor unlocked the door to the kitchen. She glanced around and saw nothing amiss. Cheddar was sitting politely with his striped tail wrapped around his feet, as if to say, "You're a little late, but I'm a good boy and I'll wait serenely for my dinner."

Oscar wandered in and gave Taylor the look. She was late and yes, he had noticed, but decided to grant her clemency.

"What a good boy," Taylor said patting his silky head. "You're no longer trashing the kitchen when I'm a smidgen late. What a personal growth moment for you." She picked him up and smooched his head making kissing noises. As she cuddled him, Oscar turned his face to her with one eyebrow raised. Taylor had the feeling she was embarrassing him.

"Okay," she said. "I get it. Enough of the awkward display." She set him on the floor.

Quickly, Taylor went through the ritual of preparing dinner for her cats. Each received a dollop of yogurt and a measured amount of canned cat food. They loved the yogurt and ate it first. It helped to diminish projectile vomiting which Oscar was inclined to do. Taylor had wondered if it was more of a statement. The result, use fewer paper towels, a species Oscar seemed intent on eradicating.

"Aw," Taylor said. "I do have a peaceable kingdom. You guys enjoy."

In the dining room, she dropped her case on the table and went to change in her room.

"Oh my!" she exclaimed, hands covering her mouth.

Scattered over much of the floor were the remains of what had been a cardboard box. Brown bites of the carton were in a large pile of discards. Several pieces had made it to her bedspread. She picked those up and added them to the heap on the floor. On hands and knees, Taylor gathered the Oscar-sized cardboard chunks. The bottom of the box was all that was left intact. It had contained her safety lights but now it was rubbish.

"Oscar!" Taylor shouted. "Very funny." But she knew she was outfoxed once again by her cat. That precious little brown feline always found a way to put her in her place. And somehow, she still easily loved him.

"Oh well," she said to the empty room. "It's not as bad as barf."

Once she was finished with dinner, a salmon salad with hard-boiled eggs and spring potatoes on a chef's blend plate of lettuce she grew herself, she sat down with her manuscript. The envelope fell to the floor.

"What on earth is this?" she said to Cheddar who was napping next to her. "Probably another wannabe mystery novelist; might as well take a look."

A single sheet of copy paper was inside. Taylor opened the folded note and read it.

Evening delivery job. Call this number. It was followed by a number in the 505 area code that indicated it was a Santa Fe or Albuquerque. *Must reply by tomorrow.* Someone had gone to the trouble to add a bit of click art on top that depicted a car with the trunk open. It could have been any flyer announcing a job opening.

"This must be for someone else at the office," Taylor said. She checked the envelope again and found it was addressed to her. The envelope and the note were computer written. There was no handwriting on it.

Cheddar blinked at her, stretched and went back to sleep. Oscar jumped on the coffee table, sat down primly and watched her. He had this way of leaning slightly to the side when he was listening to his person. Right now, his person sounded perplexed.

Taylor picked up her phone and called Jim.

"Hello Taylor dear," he answered.

She told him what she held in her hand.

"That's very strange," Jim said. "What kind of delivery job? And why you?"

"Questions I'd like answers to as well," Taylor said.

"Two things," Jim said. "Call the number and find out what it's about or ignore it. Could you do that?"

"What? Ignore it?"

Jim could practically hear the wheels turning in Taylor's head. She couldn't resist a mystery and this certainly was one.

"I'm going to call the number," she said.

"Thought so," Jim replied. "Let me know what you unearth."

Taylor sat for several minutes wondering how she would handle this and what she would say. Anita had been working a delivery job and was now missing. Taylor was more curious as to why she was left this message than anything.

She dialed the number after first hiding hers.

"Yeah?" a man answered.

"This is Taylor Browning. I received a flyer from you," Taylor said. "Why?"

"Aren't you part of the book club?" he asked.

"Yes," Taylor went with it. She was technically an honorary member.

"We have several members delivering for us," he said. "We're recruiting new drivers. Are you interested?"

Taylor was curious to know who the other members were, but thought she'd go slowly with the conversation.

"What would I be delivering?" she asked.

"Food items," he said. "For local restaurants and wholesalers."

"How much time would it entail?" she asked.

"A few evening hours two to three times a week," he replied. The man sounded as if he was the real deal, but Taylor was suspicious. She could hear clamor in the background. It sounded like someone banging things on metal. There was so much noise; it was difficult to sort it. And someone in the background yelled but it was indistinguishable. It could be a bar or a warehouse. She couldn't even be certain of the voice's gender.

"May I gave this some thought and check my calendar?" she asked.

"Sure," he said. "Call me back if you want to go forward. We pay well."

"For whom should I ask?"

"It's Michael," he said, no last name offered. "Leave a message if I don't answer."

"Okay," Taylor said. "Thank you."

She sat there holding the phone and pondering the conversation.

Her next call was to Victor.

Chapter 36

"Yes. Taylor?" Victor sounded sleepy.

"I'm sorry, did I wake you?" Taylor asked.

"Uh no, I was making coffee and had to chase down my cell," he lied. He had been napping after being out until the wee hours.

Taylor told him about the note and the telephone call with Michael, no last name.

"He said other members of the book club were delivering for him," Taylor said. "I'm an honorary member, but show up on their member list."

"So maybe it's a legit call," Victor said. "Or maybe the whole thing is a fabrication to get you involved. I don't like it."

"Me either," Taylor said. "But it might be an opportunity to find out what is going on. I had no idea there were other members of the book club involved."

"There might not be," Victor added. "That could be a ruse to make you feel more comfortable about joining their operation."

"What should I do?" Taylor asked.

"Knowing you," Victor cleared his throat. "I suspect you can't resist. But you're a civilian; I can't encourage you or tell you not to – unless it's illegal. Like that would carry any weight."

Taylor ignored the remark.

"I'm not certain I want to," Taylor said.

"Let me say this," Victor replied. "If you decide to do this truly unwise thing, please have someone with you or following you. And for heaven's sake, stay off Devil's Road. Okay? Are you hearing me?"

"Yes Victor," Taylor said. "I hear you. And thanks for the advice."

"Taylor," Victor said. "Please be careful. I don't want you to go missing too, or worse."

Chapter 37

When Gerald Barker woke in the night, he felt worse than usual. His stomach was doing flip-flops. Between the dizziness and the nausea, he fell to the floor when he tried to get up. The drugs and lack of food had to be why his trousers were so loose around his waist. He knew he was going to vomit and tried to drag himself away from his bed. He got about three feet before it came up. He felt evener weaker than a few moments ago. He passed out.

That's where his captor found him when he arrived with energy bars and water.

"Hey man," he said on the phone. "The guy's passed out."

"Are you saying he's dead?" the other voice replied.

"No, but he will be if we don't get him out of here."

"That's just what I needed; another problem to deal with."

"Not doin' anything for me either."

"We can't let him die. That would be murder and we aren't in it for that."

"What about the woman?"

"We had nothing to do with that."

"Pack him up. Then, get out of there."

"Man, I can't lift him myself."

The man at the other end swore and said, "It's not like I have nothing else to do. I'll send help. He should be there 30 minutes. Have Barker hooded and drugged. I don't want him waking up."

"Right boss."

About an hour later two men carried Barker a short distance and packed him into a van.

"Drive around a while."

"Why?"

"Just do it!"

The van stopped along 63A as the sun's first rays pierced through the trees. No cars were visible. The two men rolled Barker out onto Devil's Road and left.

Barker tried to catch his breath after it was knocked from him. The landing had been hard. He groaned and tried to move his hands. Nothing. They were tied behind him. He was blindfolded. In an attempt to remove the covering from his eyes, he scratched the side of his head. It hurt, but he didn't care. Maybe he would recognize where he was. It took several minutes of rubbing his head on the rough gravel to pull the hood off.

Although it was early in the morning, the diffused light hurt his eyes. As they adjusted, he looked around him rising up on one shoulder to get a better view.

It was an unimproved road with woods on either side. Barker thought it must be one of the forestry roads firefighters used to access wildfires. If he could stand up, he still wouldn't know which direction to go. But he couldn't. His legs wouldn't cooperate. The drugs were still in his system and he didn't have enough energy to get to his feet.

Barker struggled to reach the edge of the road. Should someone not see him, they could run him over. Every muscle in his body ached but he finally reached the ditch. His breath came in gasps; exhausted by the effort.

As he recovered, he heard a repetitive sound like an animal walking on the road. That was all he needed. Maybe an elk would butt him into the ditch; a fine finish to his life.

* * *

Juan Gonzáles, Jim's friend, was out for an early morning ride. He had been riding 63A every day since the woman went missing. He was losing hope, but he wasn't a quitter. Easy in the saddle, he listened to the leather creak and the clip-clop of his bay's hooves. Soon the pavement ran out and they were on dirt and gravel. The ride was a little less smooth, as his horse picked his way around the large stones.

The horse stopped, head up, ears on point.

"What is it boy?" Juan looked around.

Ahead, something was lying by the road. It looked like a body.

"Come on boy," he said and nudged the horse with his heels. It complied reluctantly.

When he reached the person it wasn't who he expected. It was a man. Juan bounced down off the horse and dropped the reins on the ground so the horse wouldn't move.

Juan rolled the man over. He knew who it was; everyone did. He also knew he'd been missing. He grabbed Barker's wrist and felt for a pulse. It was weak. Barker opened his eyes and tried to speak, but couldn't make words.

Gonzáles pulled his cell out and called 9-1-1. No service. He tried texting them his location instead. The text sent according to the phone, but he couldn't be certain. It was on him to get Barker to a hospital.

It wasn't easy, but he believed Barker knew he was trying to help. His arms tried to reach up and grab the saddle, but he couldn't do it.

Juan pushed and lifted until he was across the rear of the horse. Once there, he took his rope from the saddle horn and tied Barker on the best he could. He then climbed into the saddle carefully, taking care not to hurt the man further. The bay turned toward Pecos.

"Mr. Barker," Juan said, not knowing if he could hear him. "You do your best to hold on. If you can, hold that rope I tied around you. I'm grabbin' your shirt to hold you in place. We'll get you to help."

Barker did as he was told. The rope was rough but he was so relieved someone was rescuing him.

Juan clicked his tongue and the bay took off at a canter. It was a more comfortable gait than a trot. He hoped Barker didn't bounce off onto the road.

Chapter 38

The Pecos Valley Medical Center was an urgent care facility. It had recently opened. While small, it was well-staffed and at this time of day empty of patients. They hooked Barker up to fluids and checked him for broken bones and obvious injuries until the ambulance arrived that would take him to a Santa Fe hospital.

Juan stood in the waiting area while they worked on Barker. The San Miguel County sheriff walked in, saw Juan was the only one there, and approached him.

"Sheriff Connor," he said, holding out his hand. "You brought Barker in?"

"Yes," Juan told him. "That's me."

"What happened," the sheriff asked.

Juan began his story from his daily rides looking for the missing woman to riding to the urgent care for treatment. He tried to hurry because the sheriff smelled badly of cigarettes. His fingers had that yellow tint of a life-long smoker and his teeth were brown. The sheriff pulled out a pack from his light plaid shirt pocket and tapped out one – for before or after he left the clinic? And then, he added matches from his Levi hip pocket. He didn't light it.

"Okay," the sheriff said, a man of few words. "Be in touch if necessary." He wrote down Juan's name in a small notebook.

By the time the door closed behind him, the cigarette was lit.

The ambulance backed into the bay and Barker was transferred to it. As soon as Barker was safely inside they ran hot for Santa Fe.

Juan left too. His horse had obediently waited for him near the door. He mounted and headed home. Devil's Road held no more secrets today.

In Santa Fe, Presbyterian Hospital prepared for the arrival of the prominent businessman. Det. Sanchez came through the doors and checked in with the desk in the ER.

"Do you have an ETA on the ambulance bringing in Gerald Barker?" he asked the receptionist. She sat behind a counter working an impressive call station.

She picked up the phone and asked the same question of someone else.

"About ten minutes," she answered.

"Thank you," Victor said.

He stood in the crowded waiting room, not wanting to sit. Victor wasn't accustomed to idle moments. His thoughts turned to selling his house. It had been a difficult decision. Some of the best experiences of his life had happened there. Christmas with his family, cookouts with his cop pals and watching his daughter take her first steps. Yes, leaving was going to be tough, but it was time. He hoped his agent found a buyer soon.

The gurney transporting Gerald Barker came through the emergency room doors interrupting his reflection. From his vantage point, Barker looked quite pale and wasn't moving. Victor returned to the reception.

"I'll need to see the patient just brought in," he said showing his badge.

"I'll buzz you back, but check with his doctor before talking with him," the receptionist said.

"Thanks." Victor walked through the sliding doors.

He knew the drill, where to wait, about how long it took for the staff to check vitals and let him know if he could talk with the patient. Patience wasn't one of his virtues.

Taylor's call regarding the transporting job irked him. But he knew better than to take the direct approach with her. That made her only more determined to do whatever. He had a bad feeling about it.

The door to the treatment room opened and a young doctor came out. To Victor, he looked about fifteen. It seemed everyone was looking younger.

"Hi Detective," the boy-doctor held out his hand. "I'm Dr. Weber.

"Mr. Barker is badly dehydrated," he continued. "We're giving him fluids. He mumbled that he had been drugged, in his water, I think. He's difficult to understand. We're doing blood tests to determine what drug. You can talk with him briefly."

"Thanks Doctor."

Victor passed through the doors and waited near the bed as a nurse adjusted Barker's drip. She nodded.

"He said he wanted to talk with you," she told him.

Barker looked ashen, but was moving about a bit.

"Mr. Barker. I'm Det. Victor Sanchez with the Santa Fe Police. Do you feel up to answering a few questions?"

"Yes," Barker said, but his voice didn't convey the same confidence. It was probably habit. Successful people always led with strength.

"Were you abducted?" Victor asked.

"Yes," Barker said. "I don't remember ... when, but it was at my house. I ... was leaving. A meeting." The dehydration made his mouth dry and chapped his lips. The drugs must have made his head hurt and thoughts kept getting jumbled as he tried to organize them.

"Where have you been held?" Victor asked.

"Don't know. Put drugs in my, uh, water," Barker replied. His eyes kept closing. He was struggling to keep them open.

Victor asked one more question.

"Do you know why you were abducted?"

"Uh ... no," he said. "Sorry." Barker's eyes closed.

"Thank you Mr. Barker," Victor said, but the man was sleeping. There would be nothing more gained at this time. He left the hospital.

Walking across the parking lot, his phone rang.

"Sanchez," he barked.

"Det. Sanchez, Chloe Valdez here. I think I've found you a town-home. When would be a convenient time to look at it?"

This was the call he'd been both dreading and anticipating.

"I'm off duty this evening."

"Great. I'll text you the address. How about 6:00 p.m.?"

"Sounds good."

Victor sat in his car and wanted to cry. But big grownup detectives don't do that. This was not the way his life was supposed to play out. If so, his family would still be with him, his daughter would have gone to college. He and his wife would have grown old in the house they picked out together. He tuned the radio to a local Spanish music station, turned up the volume and drove away.

Chapter 39

At six he pulled into a townhome addition on the south side. He had to admit it looked nice. Individual houses lined the curving streets with lovely desert landscaped yards. The front yards where mostly gravel, but done using various colors of rocks and pebbles in flowing patterns. Chamisa and piñon, both native, had been planted or saved during construction. Many had brightly colored Talavera pots in front of the houses with flowers cascading over the rims.

He saw Chloe Valdez waving at him from in front of a house. A red sport Lexus was parked in the driveway in front of the two-car garage. She must do pretty well at this, Victor thought. She'd been driving a Mercedes last time he saw her.

The house looked like all the rest with faux adobe construction. That really wasn't a bad thing, not many developers used real adobe bricks in their design anymore. But it had the pueblo look with the flat roof and the rounded corners he wanted. The color was a soft medium brown. He wouldn't have to repaint. He parked next to Chloe's car and got out. The sidewalk took him to a courtyard. It was walled and had an iron gate with a lock. Next to the gate was a doorbell and intercom. There were several planters scattered around the courtyard the former owners must have left behind. If he couldn't use them, he knew Taylor would like the colors and she loved gardening.

"Hi Victor." Chloe shook his hand. "What do you think?"

"It's nice," he replied. Victor looked up to check out the *canales*. The wood gutters looked in good shape. The *lintel* over the *portal* also passed his inspection as did the supporting posts. He ran his hand over the exterior plaster. There were no obvious cracks. The plaster guys knew what they were doing.

"Let's look inside," Chloe said.

Inside Victor saw it had the two features he'd asked for; a fireplace and Saltillo tile floors. He didn't like carpet; it was high maintenance. He was a cop on 24-hour call. Not much time for shampooing rugs. There was a pony wall in the foyer to direct traffic. He knew that it would end up with jackets draped over it and mail deposited on top.

The living room kiva was the focal point. It was a signature feature in many Santa Fe homes. This one had a lizard painted on it as though scurrying up the chimney. Mexican tile topped the raised hearth giving it a finished look.

They walked through an arch into the dining room. Mostly a blank rectangle, they moved on to the kitchen. In there, sage-colored cabinets hung from the walls. White tile topped the counters and backsplash. Scattered Talavera blue birds accented the backsplash breaking up the white.

Victor liked it but knew he'd probably never make more than a TV dinner. Maybe he'd go upscale and get some microwave dinners from Natural Grocers.

"To your liking thus far?" Chloe asked.

"It is," Victor replied.

Chloe looked at Victor's handsome face and saw pain. She knew he was a widower. She'd sold houses to others who had lost their spouses;

they had the same expression. She thought is must take a lot of courage to leave the memories behind or maybe some people couldn't live with the ghosts. Either way, starting over had to be difficult.

"Let's look at the bed and bathrooms." She showed him the way.

There were two bedrooms and baths. The baths had similar tile to the kitchen, but the accent tiles were birds of brown and green. The bedroom floors were hardwood, but the bathrooms had more tile.

Chloe showed him the closets and storage areas. A washer and dryer were located next to the door leading to the garage.

"The furnace is in this closet," Chloe opened it. Victor nodded.

"And there is an AC unit in the side yard," she added.

"I haven't had AC before," Victor said.

"With climate change, builders are adding AC," Chloe said. "As you know it wasn't really necessary until a few years ago. But I think it will become essential. Of course, it only adds to the climate woes."

"Can't win, can we?" Victor said. "I won't use it much."

"The outside space is small and easy to take care of, but if you want to grow flowers or a few chiles, you can," Chloe said as she opened the slider and stepped out on the brick patio. "I know you're interested in security," she said. "The sliders have anti-lift locking bars and grills for an additional cost. They're available in black, white or tan if you want those added."

"How about the windows?" Victor asked.

"Impact resistant double-pane windows and heavy-duty locks," Chloe said. "You can add your own security system."

Victor was quiet for a few moments, looking at the silhouette of massive Sandia Peak in the direction of Albuquerque.

"I could use a table out here," Victor said. "It's the right side to watch the sunsets; when I get the opportunity."

From Chloe's point of view, that remark was an indicator he could see himself living there.

"Is it for you? Or should I continue looking?" Chloe asked.

"No, no more looking. You've found it," Victor said. His chest tightened as he made a big decision without his wife who had always been his sounding board. But now he was on his own and all the decisions were his. He missed her input. This would have been fun with her. But as it was, he was only buying a house.

"You sure you don't want to look at more houses?" Chloe asked.

"No," Victor said. "I like this one."

Chloe knew better than to try to persuade someone who was certain. Usually, it was helpful for people to see several options, but Victor had lived in Santa Fe for years. He knew what he wanted.

"I have the paperwork to make an offer." Chloe pulled the offer form from her portfolio and placed it on the kitchen counter. "What do you think of this amount?"

Victor knew that houses went fast, despite the high price tags on many of them. This one was moderately priced, for Santa Fe, but he still might end up in a betting war. Chloe had made the offer more than the asking price in an attempt to persuade the owners.

"It's okay," Victor said. He signed the paper.

"I'll let you know as soon as I hear from the owner." Chloe shook his hand. "And the good news is I've had several serious lookers for your house. I expect an offer soon. You should make arrangements for a mover."

"Okay," Victor said.

During the drive home, Victor thought about how much of his life had occurred in that house. But it had been several years since his wife and daughter were killed by a drunk driver. Sometimes it was too painful for him to live in it. He couldn't change the past, so he had to move on into his future. He was the kind of man who made a choice and stuck with it. Recriminations were futile and would never return his family. He'd decided months ago it was time to buy a new house, but contacting the realtor had taken a little longer.

He'd already hired a mover. They were waiting on him to give the word. The past few months he had given away what was left of his wife's and daughter's possessions with the exception of a few small things they had cherished. Much of his furniture was now sitting in the warehouse of the Santa Fe Habitat ReStore. He hoped it would find new families who could use them. People who had much less than he did. There wasn't much left to move: his basic furniture, clothes, books, legal papers and some photos. There weren't a lot of pots, pans and dishes to put away in that new kitchen. He'd cleaned that out too.

It would almost be like starting from scratch. He liked that idea.

"Yeah," he said aloud. "This is scratch."

Chapter 40

Taylor picked up her phone, thought a moment and put it back down. She was ambivalent about taking the delivery job, but still wanted to see what Anita had been doing. Unfortunately, it might have cost her life. She picked up the cell and called Jim.

"Hello beautiful," Jim answered.

"Jim," Taylor said ignoring his flattery. "I'm about to do something that's stupid and I want to ask you a questionable favor."

"My favorite kind. Do go on."

"I'm going to take this delivery job. Would you consider going with me?"

"When have I ever denied you anything?" Taylor could almost see the sneer on his face.

"Well, you're not fluent in desperate sign language."

"When are you ever going to let that go," Jim teased.

"Uh, never."

"Okay, I can live with that. When do we go undercover?"

"Undercover?" Taylor asked.

"That's what I'd call it," Jim said.

"I'll let you know." She hung up.

Before she could call the number, her phone rang.

"Rebecca, how are you?"

"Taylor, it's awful. The club members are turning on one another again. It's like they've divided into two groups. A splinter group is taking a hard line and wants to continue with the club. The rest are too afraid to come to meetings."

"That's so sad," Taylor replied. "I thought you had suspended meetings except at your home?"

"Pablo Castillo has frightened so many of our members with his nearly constant criticism of the police department. I know he's had some run-ins with the law. I wish he'd leave the group, but I don't know – and I am frankly afraid to ask him."

"Rebecca, remember what happened to Gladys."

"How could I forget? I've got Jethro her dog right next to me. I couldn't bear to take him to the shelter, even though it is no-kill. I love dogs and brought him home with me."

"That's kind of you," Taylor said. "He must have felt so abandoned."

"Not now, he doesn't," Rebecca added.

"Do you think Pablo could have killed Gladys?"

"I don't know." But it had crossed Taylor's mind.

"MacTavish," Rebecca continued. "He's no better than Castillo. His comments about former FBI cases are scaring people too. He's not as volatile as Castillo, but his arrogance and know-it-all attitude is off-putting. I don't know what to do."

"It might be better if you put the group to a vote on disbanding the club until we know what's going on."

"It makes me sick," Rebecca said. "I used to love the club. Reading is so much fun and we had such great discussions, but it's gotten to be too much with Anita's disappearance and Gladys' death. How does this even happen?"

Taylor wanted to be a good friend, but she was as much in the dark as anyone.

"May I make another suggestion?" Taylor asked.

"Sure."

"There may be new evidence soon that will help clear up everything. I can't tell you what as yet, but it would likely be best if you stopped meeting until this is over. And stay away from Castillo. He's a loose cannon. I don't trust him."

"Okay. I'll do it. I can't take the stress anymore; all the squabbling. Thanks Taylor," she added. "I think I knew what to do but I wanted someone to agree."

"Anytime."

"Goodnight."

Taylor gathered her courage and dialed the number on the flier.

"Hi, this is Michael."

"This is Taylor Browning." She cleared her throat. "I'd like to take the job."

"Great," he said. "We pay $500 cash per night for about five hours driving time. You don't have to load or unload. There will be people there to do that. Just pick up the chiles and take them to two of our restaurants. Are you available tomorrow night?"

"Uh, yes," Taylor stammered.

"Okay. Pick up at the address I'm texting you. Go around back at 6 p.m. They'll have it ready. Back up to the door with the chile painted on it. Then deliver them to our restaurants in Española and Pojoaque. I'm texting you the names and addresses. You'll get paid in Pojoaque so deliver there last. Send me a text after the last drop off so I know the deliveries have been made. That's it."

"Okay," Taylor hesitated. He sounded on the up and up. "Thank you."

She rang off and checked for the texts. The address for the chile pickup was a few blocks off Central Ave. in Albuquerque. Taylor was glad that Jim would be with her as she wasn't familiar with the Duke City.

Chapter 41

Jim agreed to ride shotgun on her chile run. Taylor thought maybe too agreeable. He seemed to think it would be a great adventure. She wasn't so sure.

She thought about it as she looked about for the right outfit. What does one wear to deliver chiles to restaurants? Taylor chose some dark clothing: dependable jeans, black tee and a dark brown jacket as it could be cool at night.

With the cats all settled in for the evening, she left hoping nothing would be destroyed on her return. She counted on Cheddar to be company for Oscar, but they were not fast friends yet. One day Cheddar took a hesitant step to join Oscar in his bed, but Oscar wasn't receiving that day. Cheddar had obviously cuddled with other cats before and thought it okay but his Aby pal wasn't so inclined. She expected that would improve with time. But would there ever be enough time for that kind of acceptance?

After collecting Jim, the two set off for Albuquerque. It was about an hour's drive, plus 10 minutes or so depending on traffic. Since it was beyond rush hour when I-25 could become a parking lot instead of a highway, Taylor planned on making it an expeditious errand.

As it happened, traffic wasn't bad. Taylor took the Central exit and drove east. Central Avenue is Albuquerque's segment of the historic Route 66. It was the revered Mother Road before the interstate system came to be and bypassed all the mom-and-pop businesses. Those included creatively styled motels along the way from teepee inns to those with flamboyant neon signs.

"What's the address?" Jim asked.

Taylor handed him her cell.

"It's the most recent text," she said.

Jim looked at it, startled.

"Do you know where this is?" he asked.

"Yeah, it's off Central about three blocks."

"Taylor, this is the worst address in the city of Albuquerque."

"It is a warehouse," Taylor replied. "They usually aren't in the best neighborhoods."

"Well this neighborhood is called the 'War Zone.'"

"What?" Alarmed.

"I've been there a few times," Jim said. "The place was trashy, including used needles and I must have seen three drug deals while there. It has the highest violent crime rate in the city. I stopped going to the State Fair years ago because it's smack-dab in the middle of it. Of course, the visitor's center calls it the 'International District' in their brochures, but no one in their right mind would want to visit it."

"Geez Jim, you're scaring me." Taylor unknowingly slowed her SUV and began looking around for trouble.

"Oh, we're okay for now," Jim said. "Central goes by the University of New Mexico and Nob Hill before it reaches the 'War Zone.'"

The UNM looked quiet as they passed. She could see the Communication and Journalism School. A few students were out and about, but the Frontier Restaurant across the street was hopping. The Frontier had been a popular place for both students and locals for decades. Tourists were catching on.

"Nob Hill is a Bohemian area of the city," Jim said. "If you have to live in Albuquerque, it's the neighborhood to choose."

Taylor smiled. There was a bit of snobbery between Santa Fe and Albuquerque. Both thought they were the better place to live.

As Nob Hill came into sight, Taylor could see why people liked to live there. Historic buildings had been restored. It had character and people were out walking in the evening. Good indicators of a neighborhood where people enjoyed living.

The street art was fabulous. Intricate colorful murals covered some of the shops and restaurants. Taylor found it hard to drive and not look at this unconventional paradise. She vowed to come back during the day and really look at it.

Unfortunately, the brew pubs, coffeehouses and neon abruptly stopped.

"Are your doors locked?" Jim asked.

"Since I backed out of my driveway," Taylor said.

Here Central looked unkempt, almost abandoned. The few people, who were out turned their back on her SUV, had hasty conversations, an awkward handshake and walked briskly away.

"See, drug deals," Jim said.

Taylor turned onto the side street where the warehouse was located. It looked like she'd taken a wrong turn in a bad neighborhood. Any available wall carried gang tagging. Some businesses and residences had high fences with barbed or razor wire at the top. The street was dusty and trashy, but mostly it was sad.

"Imagine how depressing it must be to live here," Taylor said. "This area reeks of poverty and lack of opportunity."

"Oh, they have opportunity," Jim said. "They go to work in the nicer districts and lift their cars and burgle their houses."

"Jim," Taylor said. "Being poor doesn't make you a thief."

"There it is," Jim pointed ahead to a warehouse.

"Okay," Taylor replied. "Around to the back."

She looked for the door with the chile painted on it.

"There. That one."

Jim pointed to the white door with the green chile. Time had faded the pepper. It had multiple scratches and a few dents, none of which made it at all welcoming.

Taylor turned her vehicle and backed up to the door. She got out, walked up the steps next to the loading dock and pushed the button next to the door. Jim was standing next to her car keeping watch.

"Yeah!" a man's voice crackled through the intercom. He sounded decidedly unfriendly.

"I'm here to pick up a load of chiles for an Española restaurant," she said trying not to let her voice quiver.

"No one told me there is someone new," he blustered.

"Call Michael if you want to check it out," Taylor said.

"Oh, okay," he said gruffly.

Taylor thought maybe using Michael's name clinched it. She didn't care. She took the steps down two at a time and waited by her car with Jim.

The tall door rose like one in a garage.

When the man appeared, Taylor had never had a stronger urge to run.

Chapter 42

He was big and ugly. Taylor was certain his nose had been broken at least once. Curly hair covered his head and body and protruded from his clothing everywhere it could find an aperture. He wore a white, but yellowed wife-beater smudged with unknown substances. Taylor really didn't want to give it much thought. His jeans hung low under his bulging belly.

"Easy Taylor," Jim whispered from the other side of the SUV. "Keep to business and get out of here."

"I like the getting out part." She tried to breathe normally.

Taylor opened the back of the SUV so the boxes of chiles could be set inside. The hulk carried two boxes of chiles to the end of the loading dock, set them down and went back inside.

"This is where the AR-15 would appear if I were dreaming," Jim said.

"Please Jim," Taylor gasped. "I'm in respiratory arrest as it is."

The bushy guy returned with two more overflowing boxes of chiles. After setting them on the dock, he stood there expecting them to load the shipment into the SUV.

"Michael says I don't load or unload, just drive," Taylor said.

No firearms were in sight, but Taylor had read enough mystery manuscripts to know most of the hiding places.

"I don't take orders from Michael," he snorted.

"Hey," Taylor said way too loudly. "Load the boxes into the car, or I drive away. You can explain to Michael."

He swore, but walked down the steps. Without further word, he loaded the boxes into her SUV and stalked away.

"Is that all of the boxes?" She hated to ask.

"Yup." He slammed down the large warehouse door from the inside and was gone.

Jim slid into the passenger side as Taylor started the SUV. He doubled-checked the door locks. Taylor threw it into gear and pulled away from the dock. Everyone seemed to be in a hurry on this part of Central, so Taylor topped the speed limit by a few extra MPH in an effort to get out of the War Zone as quickly as possible.

By this time the sun had set over the Jemez. She noted many of the streetlights were out. They were the old-style lights and people were stealing the copper wiring. She also noticed the small groups of mostly men were eyeing them intently; or was that with intent?

They remained quiet until the neon of Nob Hill came back into view. Taylor pulled into a coffeehouse parking lot and shut off the engine.

"Geez," she said. "I can't believe Anita did that once, let alone repeatedly."

"I've lived in New York City," Jim said. "I thought I was fearless; but no.

"Taylor, you were splendid by the way, talking to him like that," Jim added.

"It was an act," Taylor replied. "I thought if I ever had to do this again, I'd better have a modicum of respect from him. I'm still shaking."

"Do you suppose he lives in that warehouse?" Jim asked.

"Wouldn't be surprised," Taylor said. "My guess is if he does a shower isn't included."

"Yeah, but I was more worried about firearms," Jim said.

"I'll go in a get us some caffeine-free drinks," Jim added. "I'm too wired for anything else."

In a few minutes, Jim returned with a decaf coffee and tea for Taylor.

"Here," he said. "Have a biscotti."

"Oh thanks. Criminal activity always makes me hungry."

They snacked in comfortable quiet for a few minutes.

"Hate to interrupt this impromptu consumptive interlude, but we still have to deliver this to Española" Taylor started the SUV. It was a short distance back to the freeway.

When they reached the outskirts of Santa Fe, Taylor took the by-pass, also known as NM-599. It had been built to ease traffic in Santa Fe, but she hadn't noticed a difference. She turned onto Airport Road and drove into the country club parking lot.

"Okay, I give up," Jim said. "Why are we at the country club? It's not on the list of deliveries."

"Nope, but I'm not going another mile without checking the chiles for contraband."

"Bloody right," Jim said in his best British accent, which wasn't that good. "Why didn't I think of that? I can confirm, however, they smell a lot like a carload of chiles."

Taylor opened the back, picked up a tarp and spread it on the ground. She and Jim pulled out one of the boxes. They set it on the tarp and picked through it. Within minutes, most of the chiles were out of the box.

"I don't see anything," Taylor said. "Just chiles."

"Let's check another one," Jim said.

The next search produced the same result; nothing hiding among the green chiles.

"So, it's a box of chiles," Jim said. "That would eliminate smuggled goods as an option."

"This is what they call the Mayan Death Pepper?" Taylor held one up in the light of a street lamp.

"Yes, I presume so," Jim replied.

"Let's eat one and see how hot it is," Taylor said as they returned the box to her SUV.

"I'm dying to try it," Jim said. He bit off a healthy piece and began to chew.

Taylor waited. Jim was a connoisseur. She was a neophyte. If he couldn't eat it, she sure couldn't.

"It's hot; but doesn't top the Scoville scale. Here, I think you can take it." He handed it to her.

She carefully bit off a small amount. At first, it was very good, crisp and flavorful, but as she continued to chew and the oil coated her mouth, it set off her taste buds.

"Yikes! Hand me the water."

"No," Jim said.

"What do you mean no?" Taylor said with emphasis.

"That will spread the fire around," Jim explained. "Eat another biscotti. It will soak up some of the oil. There's a reason tortillas are a frequent accouterment to chiles."

Taylor ate the biscotti with fervor, grabbed another. After a few minutes, the burning took its leave.

"I can see how it would be delicious in dishes," Taylor commented. "But as much as I enjoy a little heat, that was a bit much."

"Sorry, my dear." Jim couldn't stop the wicked facial expression. He didn't much try.

The remainder of the delivery proceeded as planned. They dropped off chiles at both restaurants in Española and Pojoaque. Both cities were small and businesses lined up along the highway that passed through them. If they had proper downtowns, they didn't see them.

Taylor picked up her cash at the last stop and they went home. After pulling into her garage, she opened the back of her SUV so the chile fragrance would disburse.

As she got ready for bed, she watched the local news replay on their website. The headlines made her stop and watch.

"Businessman and entrepreneur Gerald Barker was discovered by a Pecos citizen out for an early morning ride," the coiffed blonde anchor began. "Juan Gonzáles found Barker lying on Pecos County Service Road 63A, also known locally as Camino Del Diablo or Devil's Road. You'll remember the Wine and Crime book club president and employee at the Pecos National Historical Park, Anita Juárez disappeared on this road and has not been found. Gladys Reyes, also a member of the book club was found dead along the same road."

"Barker is currently in Santa Fe Presbyterian Hospital and is stable," the male anchor read from his teleprompter. "He was severely dehydrated and reportedly had been drugged. A police spokesman would only say that his abduction is under investigation. Keep in mind this is an evolving story and we will keep you updated."

Taylor loved the way news anchors tried to talk directly to the viewer in their living room – or watching their cell. Their earnestness in delivering "up-to-the-minute" "late-breaking" stories amused her.

Well, at least they had found Barker alive. But would he be able to solve the mystery of the missing book club president; or was he responsible?

Chapter 43

Life at El Jardín Encantada was getting back to normal with the exception the police had posted officers to oversee the food prep. They were dressed in kitchen whites instead of police uniforms so customers would not be distressed.

The restaurant had been preparing to reopen for several days. Manager José Mendez was doing his best imitation of a drill sergeant. Food preppers and servers were giving him a wide berth lest his wrath fall on them.

Currently, professional cleaners were working over the dining rooms to wipe the fingerprints from all the tables before the staff replaced the table linens. The police had spread fingerprint dust all over the place. Steam cleaners had been deployed to make the floors spotless. In the kitchen, the staff did the same to the stainless steel counters, the surface of the appliances and in the pantries extra work was being done to clean and restore supplies. Trucks had been arriving all day bringing the ingredients to concoct the dishes that made the restaurant a legend in its own time.

Head chef Michael Grady was in his office working on a special menu for their grand reopening. While Miguel Velasco, the restaurant's sous-chef, worked to get his area pristine for tomorrow's food prep.

"Someone to see you," a server said to Señor Mendez after he returned from a smoke. The staff never addressed him as José.

"Where?" José asked.

"Out back." He motioned. The staff was supposed to smoke on the north side of the building where the deliveries were made, but some preferred the wooded area at the far side of the outdoor dining.

José looked out the small bar-covered window and saw a man standing among the trees. He appeared to be smoking too as a small fog hovered around him. As José crossed the pavers of the patio, he gave a hard look to all the tables. It was a lovely place to dine. Trees, a couple of large 100-year-old cottonwoods and assorted Russian olive and aspen provided shade to diners in the warm months. In the evening, lights decorated the trees in soft blue and amber. The dining area was surrounded by an adobe wall topped with farolitos that glowed softly. It was a beautiful, romantic way to dine. Instead of the formal white linens in the main dining room, these tables would be clad in southwest colors of sand and turquoise. Each table was lit with an amber candle to heighten the dreamy feel.

José opened the back gate continuing his rapid pace to reach the waiting man. He had a lot more to do than spend his time indulging in pitter-patter. There was a restaurant to open.

But as he approached the man, he slowed down. He knew who it was. This was a meeting he didn't want.

He stopped short of the cloud of smoke.

"You wanted to see me?" José said.

The man took a slow draw off his pipe, let it engulf his lungs and exhaled leisurely.

"It's time to bring the operation to completion," he said.

"Good," José said. "I didn't want to do it anyway."

"But you enjoy the rewards," he said. "That nice car, those threads and that *braw* house in Wilderness Gate all make it worthwhile."

José ignored the taunting.

"How do we get this over with?" José asked. "I've got the police breathing down my neck. They're posting people in the kitchen to keep an eye on us."

"Send the new recruit on one last delivery."

"She just ran one for us."

"This one goes to the holding location," he said.

"I can't send her there," José said. "That pickup site in Albuquerque is bad enough."

"You aren't calling the shots here," he said.

"Fine," José said. "Anything to get this over with."

"See that it goes as planned if you want to keep livin' grand. We'll do this last delivery and I'll move my business." The man disappeared into the trees. After a few seconds, the bluish smoke dissipated.

Chapter 44

Jessica called a meeting in the conference room for 10 o'clock the following morning. Everyone at the book publishing office was atwitter. It was rarely good news when Jessica scheduled a meeting that included the entire staff, let alone at the last minute. The email had read "mandatory."

Taylor sat down on the far side of the table as she usually did. Jim followed and took the seat beside her.

"Where's Aponi?" Taylor asked.

"Haven't seen her," Jim said. "Hope Jessica hasn't already fired her."

"Not funny," Taylor replied. "The way things are going it actually could happen."

"Yeah," Jim said. "Any one of us could be next."

Taylor looked across the table and through the open doors to the reception area. Candi was placing Mission Control on autopilot. That was a rare occurrence.

"Look," Taylor pointed.

"Oh no," Jim said. "This has to be super bad. Candi never attends these things. She usually knows what goes ahead of time."

Murmuring continued around the table except for Virginia. She sat quietly keeping her own countenance. But Taylor thought she had to be concerned too. She had been a victim of Jessica's rage before.

"Virginia looks like she's bracing herself," Jim nodded at the woman sitting so erect as to betray her apprehension. Her grey hair was perfectly arranged and her brown suit was elegantly cut. Jessica had fired her once and then realized no one could replace her. The publishing house simply couldn't function without her experience and expertise.

"It looks like she's holding a chair for someone," Jim said. "See, she placed a note pad there next to her."

"Interesting," Taylor observed.

"There's Aponi." Jim waved her to come over, but she sat down next to Virginia in the saved chair.

"That's strange," he said. "I hope Jessica isn't going to make an example of her."

"We'll know soon," Taylor said. "There comes Jessica through reception."

Candi followed Jessica into the conference room, closing the doors behind her. She took the seat next to Jim.

"Do you know what this is about?" Jim asked.

"No way, I've been kept in the dark too," Candi said. "I know that Aponi and Jessica were in a closed door conference for days."

Jessica was dressed in power red with several strands of pearls resting on her chest. Her white silk cami reached unexpected depths. Taylor hoped she didn't become too agitated or she might give those girls have their freedom. Red stilettos matched her suit perfectly. Taylor thought she probably had the shoes dyed. It was an odd thing to wonder about while they all waited for whatever was coming.

At the desktop podium, Jessica opened a folder already in place for her. She cleared her throat and began.

"I have some troubling news for all of us," she said. "Aponi – you all know our new business manager – has discovered a breach in our accounting books. I might as well tell you straight out; the paychecks you were issued on Friday will be returned for insufficient funds."

There were several gasps about the table. Every eye was on Jessica who for once wasn't enjoying herself. Usually bad news was something she loved to dish out; threatening jobs was a favorite. But today, it seemed she'd turned over a new leaf, albeit temporary.

"There goes my house payment," Jim said with a groan.

Even Virginia looked stricken and it was difficult to put her off balance. Everyone had to be thinking about car payments, electric bills and groceries.

"Let's settle," Jessica took control of the meeting again.

"Aponi brought to my attention that our former business manager has, allegedly, and I say it that on advice of my attorney, embezzled virtually all Piñon Publishing's assets."

The murmur of voices changed into a cacophony of outrage and uncertainty.

"Let me finish explaining," Jessica said raising her voice to be heard while signaling with her hand for quiet.

"Our attorney is taking the lead on reporting this to the police and filing charges against the former business manager," Jessica said carefully avoiding using Penny's name. "I discharged her recently but she must have accomplished this prior to that because there wasn't time for her to do it before she left the building and the computer codes were changed. This of course means she was likely fleecing the business long before asked to leave.

"Now I know this is inconvenient at best and could be devastating for some but I've secured a loan to continue business," Jessica said. "However, I couldn't get enough financing to cover everyone's salary in full."

Another simultaneous groan from the group followed.

"So" Jessica continued. "Everyone will receive half their salary for the time being. I will go without a salary until we can secure enough capital to continue the business. I hope it won't come to this, but if we cannot obtain enough funding I may have to sell or close the business."

"Geez, that's big of her," Jim whispered.

"Let's give her some credit," Taylor said. "She is trying to do the right thing."

"Aponi," Jessica said. "Without your conscientiousness, we might not have known this for months and the situation would have been far worse."

Jessica rarely said thank you in any fashion. The fact she had come this close to the words actually spilling from her mouth was a near *milagro*.

Aponi nodded. "You're welcome ma'am." She looked as if she'd like to crawl beneath the nearest piñon. It couldn't have been easy delivering news like this to the company president.

"Everyone," Jessica raised her voice regain their attention. "There is another thing. The business manager also canceled our insurance that would have paid on an embezzlement case."

Jim whistled. "We're toast. That's why the loans. I knew we had insurance, but now I guess not."

"Well, not quite toast," Taylor said sarcastically. "I still have my evening job."

Jim scoffed.

"How could I forget that?"

"There's one more thing," Jessica said interrupting the shock and whispered conversation.

"Oh good heavens," Jim said. "There's more."

"Because of this illegal misappropriation, all books currently in the publishing path will be paused," Jessica said. "I realize this seems counterproductive but it is necessary until this is resolved because we simply don't have the means to pay for anything but partial salaries at the moment. Please contact the authors who are waiting in the wings and let them know, without telling them why. We don't want to cause gossip in the industry. That could lead to a hostile takeover and a loss of confidence."

"What should we tell them?" Virginia asked.

"Tell them it's a supply chain issue," Jessica replied. "If they persist, tell them it's difficult to acquire supplies to produce books, holdups at the printing companies, especially those out of country."

"I know one we'll have trouble with," Taylor said. "Edgar Perry. He already wants a kill fee. Now he'll insist."

"I heard about that," Jim said. "First time I can remember an author asking for that; plenty of other things, but not that."

"Okay, that's it," Jessica finished. "When I know more; I'll tell you."

"What? No sorry it happened?" Jim said. "Maybe if she came to work more often, she'd keep up."

"Wishful thinking," Taylor replied.

Chapter 45

After the meeting Taylor checked her phone and found two messages. One was from Victor and the other from someone named José. She called Victor first.

"Taylor," Victor began. "In confidence: Barker is feeling better. The hospital said that he was sitting up in bed eating tonight. I'm going over later to talk with him again. I sincerely hope he knows the reason for his kidnapping as we've got questions we need answered."

"Did you ever find out what made all those people sick at El Jardín Encantada?" Taylor asked.

"Meth," Victor said. "It will be all over the news tonight."

"But how?" Taylor asked.

"That we don't yet know," Victor replied. "Had the lab run the tests twice. Some of the crime scene guys found several small pieces of crystal meth in one of the restaurants storage rooms. Somehow, it got in the food. We've allowed the restaurant to reopen with the knowledge that we're keeping a close eye on their food prep."

"Sounds prudent."

"Two of the lab guys are already there observing." Victor explained. "The manager had plenty to say about it. When presented with his options, he chose to open."

"Uh, Victor," Taylor began. "I made the first chile run the other night. Jim went with me. We stopped on the way and looked through all the boxes and found nothing. We made the delivery, I was paid, end of story."

Victor was thoughtful for a moment.

"That may have been a test," he said. "If they ask you to make another run please notify me."

"Okay," Taylor said. "The pickup place was kind of scary, but the delivery was smooth."

"How was it scary?" he asked.

"It was in the Albuquerque War Zone according to Jim," Taylor said.

"I don't like that," he said. "Let me know if they ask you again. You might want to say no.

"Oh, by the way, I'm moving into a new place soon."

"That's great Victor."

"Yeah, it is." But his voice didn't sound happy.

"Talk soon." Victor signed off.

Next, she called José thinking it must be a wrong number.

"Yeah!" he answered.

"This must be a wrong number, sorry to trouble you," Taylor said. She was about to ring off when he spoke.

"Is this Taylor?" he asked.

"Ye-yes," she said.

"We have another delivery for you."

"Uh, I usually talk with Michael."

"He's not here and we need to assign this shipment of chiles right away," he said.

"Okay," Taylor still questioned the swift change in contact.

"We need you to pick up tomorrow night," José said. "You will be given instructions on the delivery location at that time."

"Why can't you tell me now?" Red flags were aloft in her mind. She didn't like this guy.

"We're unsure of the delivery needs right now, but by tomorrow night they will be in place," José replied.

Taylor was certain he was lying, but didn't want to make a thing of it.

Chapter 46

Victor pulled into the hospital parking lot and went inside. He waved his police badge and asked to speak with Barker.

"He's been moved to a room," the receptionist said. "Second floor, room 223."

"Thank you." Victor set off for the elevators.

Barker was watching television from his bed when Victor entered.

"Mr. Barker, I'm Det. Sanchez with the Santa Fe police. We spoke earlier but you weren't feeling well. Are you up to answering a few questions now?"

"Yes. I remember, but it's a bit hazy. Come in. Sit." He turned off the TV.

"How are you feeling?" Victor asked.

"Much better, thank you."

"We're trying to determine where you were being held after the abduction," Victor said. "Can you give me any hints? Things you might have noticed."

Barker considered a moment.

"I was drugged most of the time, but I did notice a few things," he said. "The room I was held in seemed like part of a small structure. It wasn't finished. No completed interior walls. I could see between the studs that comprised the walls. The window was large but it was covered in some kind of boards. Not lath. I could have escaped that." He paused. "Well, maybe not under the influence."

"Anything else?" Victor continued to scribble notes in his pad.

"Yes," Barker began. "From time to time I smelled roasting chiles."

"Do you have any idea the area where you were held?" Victor said.

"None," Barker said. "But I was in and out during the drive before they dumped me out. It was a very rough road."

"You were found on 63A, a county road; where two other disappearances occurred.

"Was anything said to you or did you overhear anything?" Victor asked.

"They weren't chatty," Barker said. "I wondered if they were trying not to say much so I wouldn't recognize their voices."

"Do you know we found meth in one of the storage rooms at your restaurant?"

"No!" Barker said. "That's insane."

"I'm afraid not," Victor said. "One night after you disappeared, everyone eating in El Jardín Encantada was sickened. Many had to be treated at area hospitals. Some were admitted. After our lab guys were through with it, several small pieces of meth were found in a storage room."

"That's crazy," Barker said. "That almost sounds deliberate. When I get out of this bed, I'm going to be doing some housecleaning myself."

He was so indignant about it Victor wanted to believe him. But experience had taught him not everyone who protests is blameless. He knew few criminals he'd helped put away who didn't claim they were innocent. Barker could be singing the same verse.

"Have you had any difficulty with your staff at the restaurant?" Victor asked.

"Trouble? That goes without saying," Barker said. "There's a hierarchy in food service. People are constantly shuffling to get the title they want. My restaurants are small and all available titles are not filled. In my restaurants for instance the executive chef and head chef are combined.

"I had to fire a head waiter once because he was terrorizing the wait staff below him; threatening them! Wait staff are the face of the restaurant. It's important they feel safe so they can interact well with customers.

"Those at the top of said hierarchy remind me of a sergeant yelling at his troops. They practice cooking and serving before we open the restaurants. If staff collides during the practice run, there's a lot of cursing and demeaning. During the dinner hour when customers are here the dressing down is done quietly, but it is done. Sometimes people quit in the middle of the evening it gets so bad. But nothing changes."

"Has any one person stood out as a tyrant?" Victor asked. "Maybe even come after you in some way? You are after all, to them, a rich and powerful person."

"No," Barker answered. "I'm the money guy. Without me, there is no restaurant so I'm the chap you don't smart off to."

"Okay," Victor said. "I appreciate your time. If you think of anything else please call me."

"There is one more thing," Barker said. "While they had me locked up, I heard what I thought were horses close by. I was really out of it so I might have dreamed it all, but during late afternoon before they brought me more water, I was sober enough to occasionally look out. I couldn't see them but I could hear them – the horses. They sure seemed real."

"Do you think they were wild horses?" Victor asked.

"No," Barker said. "I could hear muffled human voices too, but in the distance."

"Were there many or just a few?"

"I'd say two or more," Barker said.

"That might have been members of the search party looking for the missing woman," Victor said. "But probably you didn't dream it."

"Thank you," Victor said. "Glad you're feeling better."

As Victor walked down the hall to the elevator, he made a note to share this information with his counterpart in San Miguel County. The new information added another layer to this frustrating case; if he could believe Barker.

Chapter 47

The next morning, Taylor was filled with dread as she picked up a call from Edgar Perry. She was certain what was coming.

"Good morning Edgar," Taylor said. "What can I do – "

"You can start by explaining this email I received," he interrupted her.

"It's simple," Taylor said. "We alerted all our authors that we've had to delay printing books due to some supply chain issues."

"What kind of supply chain issues?"

He would ask.

"My understanding is paper products are in short supply, but that should be alleviated soon and we'll proceed with publication."

"I knew going with a small press was a mistake," Edgar said.

"Mr. Perry," Taylor upped her reply a notch. "This is a blip in the road. Nothing else. You might be a happier person if you took these minor inconveniences in stride."

"Minor inconveniences! Minor!"

"Mr. Perry, we are publishing your book. The cover is being created as we speak. As soon as it's complete, we could go ahead and publish it in eBook."

"I want the hardcover out first!"

"In that case, we'll have to wait for the paper supply to be rectified," Taylor said. "Some of our books are printed in other countries. We can't always predict these kinds of things."

"I'll never use this publisher again," he retorted. "In fact, I'm contacting my lawyer."

"Entirely up to you." Taylor was done with the conversation. "Goodbye." She hung up.

Maybe that code of conduct Jessica wanted for authors wasn't a bad idea. Taylor scoffed.

As the fight went out of her, Taylor felt calmer. Looking out her window at the slice of street she could see, she thanked the Universe for the lovely authors they worked with. Most were hard-working, understanding people who could accommodate the swings of publishing – which could be many and varied.

But there was always one. She stood, stretched and felt better.

She had promised Victor she would let him know when her next delivery was scheduled. Her call went straight to his message box.

"Hi Victor. This is Taylor. I'm making another delivery tonight. Jim will be with me. But a little hitch; I don't know where I'm delivering. There was a new guy, José, giving me the assignment and he said I will get more information when I pick up the chiles."

There, she had fulfilled her promise. It would likely be an easy five-hundred dollars.

Chapter 48

"Why are we in the Mustang?" Jim asked. "Not that I'm complaining. I feel super retro in this red baby."

"The SUV was low on gas, so I figured, why not?" Taylor said. "It's road-worthy, but I'm a bit worried about driving it in the International District. I read there was another murder there last night."

"Don't worry," Jim said. "We've done this once so it should be a quick in-and-out. The only time we'll be out of the car is during loading."

"I think this will be the last time," Taylor said. "We'll check the chiles again and see if there's any contraband. If not, I don't see any reason to continue. We've discovered nothing."

"Sounds like a plan," Jim said.

"Are you going to be okay with the pay cut?" Taylor asked.

"I'm certainly not happy with it, but I'm trying to look at it as temporary. I've got money saved from my exhibition. Unfortunately, my earlier success story as an artist was spent on booze and things I didn't need. Not much of that left. But I think I'll be okay. Maybe it won't be long. How about you?"

"I'm okay too if of short duration," Taylor replied. "I wouldn't be in Santa Fe at all if Dave hadn't provided for me with the life insurance. I'm grateful to him every day for this gift. I have a roof over my head and it will be really nice if I ever finish renovating."

"Ha!" Jim said. "You will never finish. You'll just start over. Reno is in your blood. And with Oscar, constant repairs may be necessary. Today it's paper towels; tomorrow doors. You know they're both made from trees?"

"Very funny Jim."

"There's Central." He said unnecessarily.

The Mustang took the exit smooth as silk.

"Look at them," Jim commented. "Those guys stopped what they're doing to watch the car. Does that happen often?"

"All the time." Taylor waved to the admiring group. "They don't even see me. It's the car." She laughed.

The 1967 Pony had garnered a lot of looks and glee from men Taylor would meet while out driving. One day she came to a stop and a newer Mustang stopped across the intersection. Even though the window tint on the car was dark, the driver did a thumbs-up close to the windshield so she could see it. It was another great experience driving the 'Stang.

Taylor appreciated her father who had bequeathed it to her. He had torn it down to the ground and rebuilt it. It was mint condition as the saying goes. While there were only lap belts for safety, she paid extra attention when out and about. It was a pleasure to drive.

Unfortunately, when they arrived in the War Zone, it was receiving attention there too.

"Good thing we're not staying around," Jim said. "This baby would be stripped inside an hour."

"Geez, you're right." Taylor glanced at the small group of men congregating on the sidewalk watching as they drove by. "We're going to make short work of this."

Taylor pulled into the parking area behind the loading dock, got out and opened the trunk. She ran up the steps and pushed the button to alert the hirsute guy she had arrived. Quickly back down the stairs; she waited by Jim.

In a few moments he appeared and raised the door. He stared down at the Mustang.

"Not sure they'll fit," he said.

"We can use the back seat if necessary," Taylor said.

When he was finished, the trunk closed over the four boxes of chiles.

"What restaurant needs the delivery?" Taylor asked.

"Place in Pecos," he said. "José will text you the address." He walked through the open door and closed it from inside.

"Man of few words," Jim said.

"I don't like this," Taylor said.

"Nor I."

They took the interstate back to Santa Fe, but bent to the east and skirted the city's south side. When they reached the Pecos exit she drove into town. Taylor pulled into a gas station and parked. She texted José's cell asking where to make the delivery.

"Perhaps we should take a look in the boxes while we wait," Taylor said.

"Agreed." Jim got out of the car and Taylor opened the trunk.

There were four boxes of chiles looking much as the last delivery. Jim lifted one from the trunk and placed it on the pavement. Taylor spread the tarp on the ground. Once the cartons were empty they checked for any smuggled goods.

"There's nothing," Jim said. "I don't get it."

"What's this?" Taylor picked up one of the chiles. "Why would they let a cut one get by quality control?"

"Maybe it got cut when it was harvested and no one noticed," Jim said.

"That's possible," Taylor agreed and picked up another. "Look, this one has a slit in it too."

"I didn't notice the first delivery having any damaged chiles," Jim said.

"But we were looking for illegal paraphernalia, not scratched and dented fruit," Taylor said.

They were about to examine more when Taylor's phone indicated a text had arrived.

"What?" she questioned. "This says to take 63A to make delivery."

"No way," Jim said. "That can't be right. That's Devil's Road."

"I'll call him," Taylor said.

No answer. She left a message.

"This is Taylor. That must be the wrong address. Can't be a restaurant there."

They looked at more chiles while waiting. Each seemed to exhibit the incision made near the stem.

"Well, let's put them back," Taylor said. "I can't explain it."

Jim was about to replace the box of chiles in the trunk when he had an idea.

"I'm going to open one of these and see if there's a reason for the slit."

Carefully, he pried the chile open.

"They'll never miss one." He tore it open with his thumbs. Something fell out onto the pavement.

Taylor picked up a tiny plastic bag containing crystals.

Jim examined it carefully, holding it up to the sun. He exhaled sharply.

"What is it?" Taylor asked.

"Crystal meth."

Chapter 49

"Meth?" Taylor asked.

"Blue meth to be exact," Jim said. "And look how much is shoved into this chile."

"Isn't that what made everyone sick at Barker's restaurant?"

"Yup," Jim observed. "And we're transporting it through New Mexico."

"Wouldn't it be labor intensive to fill all of these with meth?" Taylor asked.

"Yes, but there is such a thing as a chile corer," Jim said. "Although they usually remove the core from the stem end, with the chile slit like this, it wouldn't be that difficult to remove most of the core and then add the meth. They could get illegals to do it for almost nothing.

"It was careful work," Jim continued. "The chiles still look intact."

A text arrived.

"We have a customer who lives along 63A." José's text read.

"Can't drive that road." Taylor texted back.

"Go as far as you can. He will meet you." José replied.

"I don't like this," Jim said. "I think you ought to give Sanchez a call."

"Voice mail," Taylor said. Jim grimaced.

"Victor, it's Taylor again. Jim and I are in Pecos and the delivery guy, José, is instructing us to take 63A to deliver these chiles to an individual. I'm in my Mustang and it's not cut out for this. I was told to go as far as the car would take me, but I've got a bad feeling. We think the chiles are filled with meth. Call me back. Thanks."

"Now what?" Jim said.

"I'm going to call the station and talk with an actual person," Taylor called the non-emergency number. "More voice mail."

"The bane of the technological age," Jim said. "No human contact. No wonder loneliness is epidemic."

First she sat through more recordings and finally repeatedly punched zero until the voice system gave up and sent her to a person.

"Santa Fe Police," a man's voice answered.

"I need to speak with Det. Sanchez," Taylor said. "It's urgent."

"Maybe you need to call 9-1-1," he replied.

"Would you please listen to me," Taylor cursed the callous humans we had become. "I've left messages on his cell but there's been no response. It's important."

"Don't know what to tell you," the man said. "Sit down right over there," he instructed someone in the building. "Ma'am, he's out on a call. I don't know when he'll be back." It was said as if he was bored with her, maybe with everything.

"It's about meth trafficking," she said.

"Where is this trafficking occurring?" he asked.

"Right now in Pecos." She knew straight away that was the wrong thing to say.

"Pecos is in San Miguel County. Not our jurisdiction. You need to call the Pecos Police or the San Miguel Sheriff's office." He hung up.

"I can't believe it," Taylor said. "How rude!"

"No time to contemplate the demise of courtesy," Jim said. "Do we turn around and go home risking who knows what kind of reprisal or make the delivery?"

"I don't know," Taylor replied. "But I'm not taking this baby any farther on that road than it will easily go. I hope this guy has an SUV."

"Then I guess we have our decision. Go on as if we don't know there are drugs involved."

"Okay," Taylor agreed reluctantly. "Never expected to be a drug smuggler. What's the prison term for that?"

"You'd probably get off with probation," Jim quipped. "I'd be made an example."

"Very funny." Taylor closed the trunk on the boxes.

"Let's go," Jim said.

As they drove off a man in a truck who had been silently watching dialed a number on his cell.

"It's me," he said. "They know the cargo."

Chapter 50

Victor Sanchez was furious with himself for not charging his phone last night. He had moved to his new house over the weekend and couldn't find anything. Actually, the mover made the transition for him with Chloe overseeing the progress. He'd been called out just as they arrived and asked Chloe if she could let them in. Boxes were blocking every available electrical outlet. He had to plug in his phone to see if there were any messages. He'd been in the middle of a robbery investigation at a convenience store and it had completely slipped his attention.

Inside the convenience store he checked in with the lab guys.

"Have you finished in the office?" he asked.

"Yeah," one lab tech answered. "Please keep booties and gloves on in case we missed anything"

Victor entered the back office and looked for an outlet. There was one on the wall near the landline. He plugged in his phone and waited for it to start. Three messages; one from the precinct and two from Taylor. He hurriedly listened to them. The call from the precinct dispatcher said Taylor had called. Taylor's messages were alarming. If meth had been concealed in the chiles, she was in this up to her eye-brows. He hoped she was on her way back to Santa Fe. But knowing her, he felt that improbable.

"I've got to leave," Victor said as he walked by the checkout. "Send me your findings."

"Roger, that," the lab guy popped off. Victor ignored it, got in his police car, plugged in his phone and placed it in the holder. "Should have done that long ago," he said, disgusted with himself. He called Taylor's number, but she wasn't answering. There were two messages from her. There was a bad feeling in the pit of stomach. Something was wrong.

Once he'd checked his messages he got out of the car and instead chose the newer Ford Police Interceptor one of the other officers had parked. He was going to need something more agile if he ended up on 63A. The SUV spun some gravel as he exited the parking lot. As soon as he hit the pavement, he turned on his lights. It was going to seem like a long drive to Pecos, but his hunch told him she was not on her way back to Santa Fe. At least Jim was with her, but he wasn't sure that would be enough.

Victor plugged in his phone and headed south to 25, the quickest way to Pecos. He'd worry about the jurisdiction issues later.

Chapter 51

Taylor tried to phone Victor again, but it was useless. They had run out of bars shortly after entering the county service road.

"Still can't get him. I'm unwilling to go any farther in my car. I'm going to turn around while I can still see. For want of a better idea, we're going back to Santa Fe."

"I'm with you on that," Jim said. "Here's a good spot." He motioned to a wider area of the road.

Taylor carefully maneuvered the Mustang until it was safely facing in the direction of Pecos.

"Now, let's get out of here." Taylor put the car in drive.

"What's that?" Jim turned around and looked behind them. "There are headlights approaching. Let's go so we don't block the way."

"Why aren't we moving?"

"Because he flicked his lights at me," Taylor said. "It may be the buyer for the chiles."

"Why don't we unload the boxes and leave them," Jim asked.

"Okay." Taylor said. She quickly got out of the driver's seat and opened the trunk.

The two of them unloaded the boxes and left them at the side of the road. The approaching car was getting close and they hastened to leave. They both had their doors open when someone stepped out of the trees along the ditch.

"What's your hurry," he said with authority.

"We've left the chiles," Taylor said. "We need to go."

"It's a bit late for that," the man's voice said.

Taylor thought his voice sounded familiar, but couldn't place it.

"It's not too late," Jim said. "We've made the delivery. We're leaving."

Jim and Taylor tried to get inside the car, but his voice was commanding.

"Stop," he said. "I prefer you stay." He was a large man and he brandished a handgun. It wasn't pointed at them but rested in his hand that hung loosely at his side.

He was interrupted by the SUV arriving.

"Hey, what's the deal?" the driver said on exiting the vehicle. He was a thin man. He picked nervously at his beard.

"This is the shipment," the man with the gun said. "There's been a snafu. It seems these two got to snooping and they know."

"Know what?" the driver asked.

"I'll help you load the boxes and then deal with them."

As the gunman walked towards the SUV Taylor said, "Should we get in the car and gun it?"

"Not enough time," Jim said. "If you work your way over here, we can disappear into the trees."

Taylor closed the door softly and walked around the front of the Mustang. When she reached Jim's side she said, "Just say when."

"You two stay right there," he demanded.

"The second he is behind the car, we go," Jim whispered. The small man was already opening the back of his SUV and couldn't see them.

Taylor watched, heart pounding, as the man carried a box jungle style to the back of the SUV.

"Now!"

There was a deep step into the ditch to reach the other side. Jim was waiting to pull her up.

"You okay?" Jim asked.

"Fine, let's go!"

Taylor thought her heart would surely explode with all the adrenaline flowing. She flashed back to that night in Sedona hanging from the side of a cliff. It had felt like that then too.

There were angry voices back at the road and she could hear them searching.

"We're making too much noise," she gasped to Jim as they slowed down.

"Yeah, we need to stop and hide for awhile. Let them get tired of looking for us."

She stopped. It was hard. Her instinct was to keep running, but they had to know where their pursuers were.

"It's going to be completely dark in a few minutes," Jim said. "Do you see a good place to hide?"

In the dimness she looked for cover.

"There!" she pointed. "That group of chamisa."

It was a short struggle for Jim to squeeze into the middle but Taylor slipped in easily. Once there, they crouched in silence. It wasn't long before they heard the two men approaching. One had a flashlight and was waving it about. Taylor covered her head with her jacket and looked away. Jim followed taking care to hide his watch so it didn't reflect in the beam of the torch.

"Do you hear them?" the driver asked.

"No," the gun toting man observed. "They may have circled back."

"I thought I heard a car a minute ago. Maybe it was them."

"Don't know how John is going to take this," the driver said.

"Oh, we're going to pay," the other said. They scrambled back through the forest toward the road.

After a few minutes of silence Taylor asked, "Do you think it's safe to go back to the car?"

"No," Jim said. "I don't. I'm afraid they'll have someone watching it."

"So we're stuck here," Taylor asked. "In the Pecos Triangle?"

Chapter 52

There was a hold up on the four-lane. It was quickly becoming a car park. Victor had his police lights on, but no siren. He'd go around, but vehicles were already waiting on the shoulder. He radioed the station.

Victor depressed the transmit button and waited two seconds to make sure the channel was open.

"Unit 2-6-0 to dispatch, radio clear?"

"Go ahead 2-6-0."

"Requesting info on I-25 at Exit 299 Glorieta/Pecos. Traffic stalled."

"DOT reports a 10-50," the dispatcher replied.

"Emergency vehicles in route?" Victor asked.

"Affirmative."

"10-04," Victor said and released the button.

If he could only get off the exit and take the road into Pecos, but he figured it would be at least a 20-minute wait. Both sides of the roadway were fenced. It was times like this Victor wished wire cutters were standard issue.

Every second he was sitting still Taylor could be in danger. He'd have to give it a go.

He turned on the siren.

Chapter 53

Taylor and Jim tried to get their bearings under the night sky. "Which way is the road?" Taylor asked.

"That way, I think." Jim pointed. "Had I been hiking normally, I would have turned around and taken some photos of what was behind me. That's always a good idea when in unfamiliar woods. But when running for my life after dark, it didn't come to mind."

"I don't hear anyone crashing about," Taylor whispered. "Maybe we could find the road, but stay inside the woods where they couldn't see us."

"With no better idea to offer, let's try that," Jim replied.

The moon was full and offered the only light to navigate through the trees. They slowly walked through the Pecos forest carefully avoiding the ponderosa pines that seem to spring at them in the murkiness. Taylor kept her arms out and slowly felt the bark of each tree as she passed it. Not only did it help her negotiate the night, but kept her from falling over roots and fallen limbs. The piñon were more difficult. Even a hundred-year-old piñon might be no higher than 10 feet. They don't grow in clumps because their roots stretch down and outwards some 40 feet in search of moisture. Since they need their space she was fairly certain there wouldn't be another one growing immediately in her path.

While contemplating the growth of trees, Taylor realized she could no longer hear Jim next to her. She stopped and listened. Nothing. Had he seen or heard something? Taylor stood quietly in case she could hear the approach of the smugglers again. There was nothing, not even a call from an owl or an elk crashing through the underbrush. Definitely, there was no Jim.

She felt paralyzed with dread. Where was he? How did they become separated? Should she keep going? Taylor wondered if this had happened to the people who had disappeared in this wild place. They must have thought they knew the direction back to the road too.

This was their point of separation. Taylor stood quietly wanting to think before doing something stupid. But hadn't she already done a stupid thing? She'd agreed to deliver the chiles and the next thing she knew her valuable car was abandoned on Devil's Road and she and Jim had plunged into the woods. Now they were split up.

Indecision can be a killer. Taylor knew she hadn't turned since the moment she realized Jim was gone. She was still facing their original direction. If they had been correct, she should keep going forward being alert for any sound. She'd gone about three metres when she heard a campfire. Maybe some hunters or campers were nearby and could help her get to the road.

At the moment she didn't trust anyone, she moved to her right in the direction of the noise. It sounded as if someone was adding wood to the fire; a small thud followed by ash and sparks spewing upwards. There was a faint glow coming through the woods as she edged toward the camp. She allowed herself to feel some relief. Help could be near. Maybe they could find Jim too.

Aware it could also be the smugglers, she set down each foot with care to avoid breaking a twig or stumbling. Finally she reached the clearing and could plainly see what held so much promise. Before she took the plunge into that warm light she wanted a good look at who was there.

A man sat on a log. He wore a driving cap and smoked a pipe. He poured a cup of coffee from a blue coffee percolator. When he replaced the percolator on the fire she could see his face clearly. It was John MacTavish from the Wine and Crime book club.

Taylor felt immediate relief. Someone she knew who had been an FBI agent. A bit of a hot head, but surely helpful in her current situation. She was about to emerge into the clearing when the two men who had threatened and chased them came out of a tent and sat down next to MacTavish. Confused, she noticed three extra cups sitting on the rack across the fire. Was there a fourth person expected? If so, who?

She clasped her hands over her mouth and crouched in the darkness.

Chapter 54

Jim stopped. Where was Taylor? She had been right beside him only moments ago.

"Taylor?" he whispered. "Taylor!"

But her voice didn't return to him.

Where could she be? He called her name twice more but got no response. Not knowing what to do but blaming himself, he turned and went back the way he'd come calling her name softly as he slogged through the woodland searching. He knew that could give him away to the two men who were stalking them.

Jim noticed a glow coming from ahead. He paused, softly calling Taylor's name. She didn't have the supplies necessary to start a fire and he didn't want to surprise the wrong person.

Taylor heard someone approaching in the trees. She eased herself into a dark space between bushes. She could still keep an eye on the campsite while observing the newcomer. Maybe it was the fourth person; the one the extra cup awaited. As he emerged from the trees into the cast off light from the flames she recognized him.

"Jim," she spoke it so softly she was surprised he heard.

"Taylor," he murmured. "Where are you?"

She reached out and touched his pant leg. He sat down beside her.

"I'm so happy to see you," Taylor was relieved.

"Are you all right? No injuries?" he asked.

"I'm fine. How did you find me?"

"Backtracked. What's the score?" He nodded toward the flickering light.

"The two guys we ran into on the chile handoff and a guy from the book club."

"Which one?"

"John MacTavish," Taylor said. "He fancies himself a Scottish Highlander. They've been drinking coffee and talking, but I can't hear what they're saying? I think they are waiting on someone. Notice the lonely coffee cup."

"Good observation," Jim said. "Shall we try finding the road again?"

"I'd like that, but I feel like we need to hear what they're saying," Taylor said. "Do you think we can get closer and not get caught?"

"I think it's worth a try. This may be the only way we know what's going on. The police will need the information for their investigation."

They edged around the clearing. When they found a good vantage point, they stopped and listened.

"I can't believe you two made such a mess of this." MacTavish was angry.

"We didn't expect them to run," the man said who had held a gun on them.

"Let the woods take care of them like the others," said the skinny guy. "It has a way of dealing with people who don't know their way around."

"Do you recognize those two?" Jim asked.

"No. Never saw them before today," Taylor said. "They aren't in the book club."

"We can't leave loose ends," MacTavish said. "Barker never saw us so he's harmless. He didn't see you, right?"

They bobbed their heads in unison. It would have been funny if it wasn't dead serious. They were lackeys. Their days were likely numbered.

"But the two lost in the woods saw both of you, yes?" Again, the obedient bobbleheads went into motion.

"Then they have to go," MacTavish said.

"Hey," the skinny guy protested. "I didn't sign up for killing."

"Then you should have concealed your identity," MacTavish said.

"What happened with that other broad?" the gunman asked.

"Confronted me," MacTavish said. "Somehow she figured it out. Seems she was some kind of super librarian; dug around until she found something on me. I didn't have a choice but to silence her. Widow. Few people to miss her."

"He's talking about Gladys," Taylor said. Her eyes brimmed with tears. "Oh, how could he? She was a lovely innocent woman."

Jim touched her arm.

"If they killed Gladys, they won't think twice about us," Jim said.

Before they could leave, MacTavish stood.

"I'm out of here," he told the two men. "Someplace I have to be."

"What are we supposed to do?" The thin man stood.

"Find them!" MacTavish snarled. Within several seconds, he was gone.

"That must be the way out," Taylor said.

"Give him a couple of minutes and we'll leave," Jim said.

"Okay." Taylor agreed.

Before they could follow MacTavish, the fourth man trudged into the clearing.

"José! What are you doing here?" One of the men asked.

"Is that the José who sent me down Devil's Road?" Taylor asked.

"Good guess," Jim whispered. "We need to get out of here. Mac-Tavish has been gone long enough. Maybe we can find the path he took."

Taylor nodded. They rose to go.

Cautiously, they put as much distance between the clearing and the three men as possible. The moon had risen and was casting a pale radiance in the deep woods. Within a few minutes Taylor and Jim found the path the smugglers seemed to be using. It wasn't a marked trail, but the underbrush had been walked on enough they could follow it if they were attentive.

"Do you think we're anywhere near the road?" Taylor asked.

"They wouldn't want to spend a lot of time hiking in and out," Jim said. "I would guess, yes, we're close."

That's when two shots rang out.

Chapter 55

Victor edged his patrol car alongside the parked vehicles, siren wailing, lights flashing. The SUV was creeping along the ditch at a dramatic angle. He hoped it wouldn't turn over, but wasn't wholly confident. He turned off the siren and used the speaker system to try to clear the highway shoulder.

"Motorists," he said. "Emergency vehicle needs access to the shoulder. Please yield." He repeated several times and inched forward. After reactivating the siren, people were at least trying to move out of the way. Despite that, his SUV scratched the side of one of the idling cars.

"Hey man," Victor dug out one of his cards, stretched his arm out of the window and handed it to the driver. "Sorry. Call me. We'll take care of it."

"Okay, thanks," the driver said. "Hope you get there in time."

It took about 15 minutes to reach the exit. Several times Victor was afraid he was going to lose his fight with the ditch and have to walk to Pecos. At times, he had to lean against the driver's window; the vehicle was in such a perilous tilt. But eventually enough cars moved over that the exit appeared and he could get off. Once on the road to Pecos, he gunned it and made up some time.

He'd been to the town many times and was familiar with 63A. He knew the stories of disappearances and those handed down by the Native people in the area. The one about the serpent was particularly vivid as told to him by his grandmother during his childhood. He hadn't given it much credence except the vanishings were real. Those people hadn't been found and he doubted they ever would be, except by a future archeologist. Unlikely endings occur all the time. Victor was well-acquainted with those.

The intersection of 63A was now in sight. He slowed down so as not to miss the turn. It didn't take long to find Taylor's red classic Mustang parked along side of the road. The passenger side door was open.

He grabbed a flashlight. Where were they? Had Taylor and Jim been kidnapped or had they entered the woods on their own? Victor walked about the car with gloved hands. When he reached the passenger side, he closed the door being careful not to touch the handle. The ground was slightly soft. He could detect three sets of footprints; hiking boots. Two sets were large and one was much smaller, such as a woman might wear.

No, he didn't like this at all.

Chapter 56

"Were those gun shots?" Taylor added unnecessarily.

"Of course they were," Jim said. "José probably came out to tie up some loose ends."

"Which means we're next," Taylor said with horror. "We've got to get off the trail."

"Come on," Jim said. "Let's go this way. It looks denser. Better to hide."

They plunged into the underbrush heedless of the noise. There was no time to be quiet.

"Here," Jim grabbed her elbow. "This looks good."

"How can you tell?" Taylor asked. "It's dark."

"It feels thick," he said. "That's what we need. Now duck down."

Crouching in the cover of the brush, Taylor tried to steady her runaway heart.

It was so silent in the forest. Taylor was afraid her labored breathing would give them away. If not for the moonlight, the darkness would be total.

"Let's move," Jim said.

They walked deeper into the forest. Something loomed ahead. It wasn't a tree or bush; much larger, low and wide.

"What's that?" Taylor asked.

"It looks like a shelter of sorts," Jim said. "Come on, let's get inside.

The shed had possibly once sheltered hunters. Jim tried the knob and the door creaked open.

"Hang on," Jim said. "I have a small light on my keychain."

It was definitely small, but mighty. It lit up half of the room. That's all there was, one room. Opposite the door was a large window. It had been boarded up. Maybe there had been damage done, but it looked like time had done most of it.

"Here, take this." Taylor handed a crystal to Jim.

"What is it? Feels like a stone."

"Black tourmaline. Rachel Blackstone gave them to me for protection."

"Them?"

"I have the selenite. Together we are protected. I hope."

Jim dropped the crystal into his jacket pocket. Taylor couldn't see him roll his eyes heavenward. Just as well.

Inside was a mess. The floor was covered in several inches of dust and debris. There was a table with an empty water bottle and a few energy bars.

"Looks like someone has been here recently," Taylor observed. "The water bottle is half empty."

A single bed occupied one side near the window. There was a very old wood stove at one end. An old stove pipe rose from the back and exited the side. But starting a fire would have been deadly. The venting had rusted through in several places. In early times, hunters must have cooked and kept warm with this stove because there was no fireplace.

Among the trash and dirt they found a chamber pot.

"That's odd," Taylor said. "I guess no plumbing so it's either this or the great outdoors."

"Sounds appealing," Jim replied.

Something caught his eye as he swung the light along the floor. He bent over to reach a piece of dark fabric. Jim held it up.

"What on earth is that?"

"Hood from a coat," Taylor offered. "Maybe someone forgot it; would be easy to do in this mess. Are all hunters this untidy?"

"There are no snaps or zipper to attach it." Jim ignored her opinion of hunters as he examined the hood. "I've watched a lot of kidnapping mysteries and this looks like a hood for that purpose."

"Do you think those men kidnapped Anita? What about Gladys?"

"I think those men would do exactly that if they had something to gain," Jim said.

"I want out of here. We don't want to be here if they return."

"Pretty sure we don't have to worry about anyone but José and MacTavish. The other two are likely dead."

Taylor pushed that mental picture out of her head.

"Let's proceed with caution back to the path," Jim whispered.

"You're the outdoorsman. I'm in lockstep with you."

After a few moments, Taylor stopped.

"What do I hear?"

"Sounds like someone coming on the path."

"Maybe MacTavish is returning?" Taylor asked. She hated to think what that could mean.

"We need to be certain who it is before showing ourselves," Jim said.

Whoever it was made no attempt to hide himself, but was crashing through the underbrush toward the shed.

They moved behind two trees and stayed motionless. Taylor carefully stole a look and recognized José. She motioned to Jim but he had already seen him. Taylor closed her eyes as he passed them on the way to the shack they had vacated only moments before. She wasn't sure why. Would he be less likely to see her with her eyes closed?

When he entered the shed, a bright light illuminated the structure sending shafts of glowing radiance through the window and the open door.

Taylor eased over to the tree Jim was hiding behind.

"What's that?"

"Maybe he has a brighter flashlight?" Jim tried. But he didn't believe it.

"I want to see," Taylor said.

"I admit I do too." Jim took her arm and they advanced slowly. Carefully, they moved to the edge of the shed.

"Take a tiny peek," Jim said.

Taylor held to the corner of the structure and looked in with only one eye. The scene was so shocking she jumped back.

"Oh no!"

"What is it?" Jim asked.

"You'll have to see for yourself. José won't see you."

Jim changed places with Taylor.

"Do you see what I saw?" Taylor asked.

"Exactly what do you think ... you ... saw?" If Taylor could see Jim's face clearly, it would have been ashen.

"That is a glowing snake! The rumor must be true. The Indian tribes are right." She was babbling.

"It's just a bright light," Jim said.

"No it's not! I saw it." Taylor pushed in front of Jim to confirm what she had seen.

Inside the room was a vast light. It appeared to come from the floor where it coiled. From there was an upright light that reminded her of a serpent. There were no discerning features so she couldn't be sure.

José stood in disbelief. He tried to back up but he appeared frozen in place.

Taylor could watch no more.

"Let's go!" she said. "I can't watch."

When they reached the trail, they stopped to listen first.

That's when Taylor heard someone calling softly.

"Taylor? Jim?"

"It's Victor!" Taylor said.

"I'm even glad he's here," Jim muttered.

They left the safety of the pines, listening for anyone else on the path.

"Victor," Taylor said. "We think someone named José shot two men."

"Where?" Victor asked.

"There is a campsite that way," Jim said. "But you won't find him there now. He's in a shed in that direction."

Taylor noticed he didn't explain further.

"Okay," Victor said. "Let's head back to the car. I'm going to call the Pecos sheriff's office. This isn't my jurisdiction and they'll be displeased with me."

When they reached the car, Victor called dispatch.

"The two of you get in the car and go home," Victor said. "I'll park my cruiser down the road and wait."

"For what?" Taylor asked concerned.

"For whatever," Victor said. "Either backup or I'll handle it myself. Depends on your friend José. Say, is he the José who works at the restaurant Barker owns?"

"I think so." Taylor replied. "He did assign me this chile run."

"All right," Victor said. "You two go. Make sure she gets home safely Jim. I'll check in after this goes down."

"Will do." Jim didn't argue.

The car accident had been removed from the east bound side of the highway. Few people were out and about now as Taylor drove toward Santa Fe. The ride home was mostly quiet. The odor of chiles still permeated the car. It was usually a welcome aroma, associated with good food and fellowship. Taylor hoped it would someday mean that to her again, but today it was linked to fear and murder.

The word *intruder* kept coming to mind as she drove. It appeared as if a printed message across her mind. She didn't know what it meant but she couldn't shake it. Images of her house's interior kept forming in her mind. Oddly, her perspective was from the floor of her house. In one, she could see what appeared to be men's shoes. Why would she see that?

This must be what happens when people have terrifying experiences, she mused.

When the lights of south Santa Fe finally came into view, Taylor sighed with relief.

"Didn't think we make it?" Jim asked.

"I admit I had moments of doubt, especially when we got separated," she replied.

"Go to your house," he said. "I'll check it out and take an Uber home."

"That's not necessary," Taylor said. But she wondered after the strange impressions she had been receiving.

"Nope," Jim said. "I promised Sanchez I'd make sure you were okay. That's what I'm doing."

"Okay." Taylor knew she would lose this argument. No sense continuing.

She pulled into the garage and let down the door.

"It's good to be home," she said.

But as they entered the house, she had a bad feeling. Taylor pushed it away. It was just residual anxiety from their fright. Or was it confirmation of the persistent thoughts or visions she had during the return trip? She brushed the weird notions away. Everything appeared normal at first.

"There, you see," Taylor said. "Everything is as it should be – except, where are my cats?"

Chapter 57

Taylor flipped on the kitchen light, but there were no cats.
"I don't get it," she said. "They always meet me at the door. For one thing, I'm late for Oscar's dinner."

"You're right," Jim said. "He doesn't take that lightly. I'll take a look around. You stay here."

"Why should I stay here?" Taylor was miffed at being dismissed. "I'm going with you."

"Okay, come along." Jim was miffed too, but Taylor didn't care. She wanted to see her babies were okay.

"We need to be careful. Remember I kept getting something about an intruder on the way here."

"Yes, so you said." Jim obviously didn't believe it.

They were entering the living room when a man stepped out of the hall and blocked their way.

"You've gone far enough." It was MacTavish!

"Where are my cats?" Taylor demanded. She tried to lunge past him, but one very strong arm pushed her back.

"Hey," Jim shouted. "Don't touch her. She's done nothing to you."

"Really, nothing?" MacTavish said. "She's done her best to ruin my operation. One I was about to move to another location."

While Jim had MacTavish's attention, Taylor felt for her phone in her front pants pocket. She carefully slipped her index finger up across the face of the cell to get to the home page. Now, where was Victor's icon? It was the second down from the top on the right side. Taylor tried to visualize where that was without being able to see the screen. It was made all the more difficult because she was frightened. Her fingers felt thick and clumsy. She took a mini-step behind Jim and took her shot.

Victor answered. "Sanchez." She could hear him, but just barely.

Jim covered for her. He even held his arm protectively in front of her.

"Then go MacTavish!" he said loudly. "Take your *operation* and leave!"

"That's the problem," MacTavish said. "You've made that a bit of a dilemma."

* * *

Victor was listening intently now. He'd been driving the speed limit, but quickly turned on his lights, but not the siren, and gunned it. He was about 20 minutes outside of Santa Fe. If only he could risk using the radio, he would alert Santa Fe dispatch to get over to Taylor's house. But if heard, that might endanger the lives of Taylor and Jim. He turned off the radio and drove silently.

He'd left the Pecos sheriff to continue the investigation on 63A. When the sheriff arrived he had been bristly with Victor and asked him to leave it to the local constabulary. Not quite in those words.

Several officers and had been searching the woods outside Pecos when he left. Victor didn't know what they had found after arriving at the campsite. The sheriff, obviously someone who had authority issues, didn't cotton to a citified detective *suggesting* what he needed to do.

Now, however, it was imperative he get to Taylor and Jim before MacTavish resorted to violence. His foot was flat on the floor as he zoomed through the darkness. Only the moon and his headlights broke through. The rotating blue and red lights gave the night an eerie disconcerting feel.

* * *

"Are you undercover for the FBI?" Taylor knew full well he wasn't but maybe he didn't realize how much she understood. Knowing that Victor could hear them she moved from behind Jim. "Did we inadvertently step into a covert investigation?"

"I think you know that isn't it," MacTavish said. "But laboring for the FBI all those years did give me insight and experience into my current business. You know well what that is. I've had people observing you. We know you searched the boxes of produce and discovered the drugs. Did you think you were dealing with amateurs?"

"Who do you get to core the chiles and insert the drugs?" Jim asked, stalling for time. "That's intensive time consuming work."

"There are people willing to work for almost nothing," MacTavish said. "These enterprises in Border States find a great number of, shall we say *staff*? And they are already accustomed to keeping their mouths shut."

"So you take advantage of migrants?" Taylor fairly spit it out. MacTavish was the worst of the worst. Why hadn't she seen it before?

"They need the money, honey." MacTavish said it so sweetly Taylor thought she would be sick.

If only they could keep him talking until Victor arrived. She had no idea if he was in Santa Fe or still in the Pecos Triangle.

"Where are my cats?" Taylor asked.

"Not to worry my dear, they are safely in your bathroom.

"But you, you are different. You have exposed my operation."

"Then why don't you leave," Jim said. "You'll have a head start. You could be in Juárez in a few hours if you hurry. We'll give you a five-hour head start."

"Well, isn't that thoughtful of you," MacTavish said sarcastically. "No, we're waiting on an associate of mine so make yourselves comfortable. Sit! I insist."

Taylor sat on her sofa while Jim chose the chair.

"Take your cells out and place them where I can see them," MacTavish ordered.

Jim set his on the arm of the chair, while Taylor carefully laid hers face down on the coffee table next to her favorite Zuni pot. She didn't want their captor to know there was an open call and Victor was listening in.

Every muscle in her body was at readiness, but for what she didn't have a clue. There was no way she could attack this large man. Even if she could screw up the courage, he would probably shoot her before she cleared the sofa.

"Who are we waiting for?" Jim asked.

"Just think of him as a closer," MacTavish said. "He ties up matters and handles cleanup."

MacTavish stood next to the ladder and the open hall that led to Taylor's bedroom and bath. Taylor watched nervously. She was certain they were the matters in need of tidying. MacTavish wanted someone else to pull the trigger.

A movement in the hall caught her attention. Both cats were standing quietly watching what was going on. Oh no, she thought.

Oscar must have let them out of the bathroom with his new trick of opening the door. She dared not say anything. The crazy Scotsman might hurt them.

"If you're into smuggling, then why on earth did you join the book club?" Taylor asked. "You surely don't enjoy reading on your days off from your *operation*. I can't see you sipping a margarita and thumbing through a book while arranging for drug deliveries or giving orders to your closer."

"I like reading. And it's good to fit into your environment; learned that in the FBI while undercover."

"How surreptitious that experience in serving our country inspired your clandestine activities." Jim was angry. Taylor recognized the reddening of his face. His fists were clenched, feet apart. He was holding back by sheer will.

"Did you kill Gladys?" Taylor tried to buy more time.

"Her research was far too good," he said. "She stumbled onto why I left the FBI prior to the regular retirement time. It was a trifling discretion but the FBI doesn't like even minor issues. They offered to let me keep my pension benefits if I would leave early.

"She made the mistake of texting me and Castillo to meet her. I intercepted her as she was driving to his house. She left me no choice."

Taylor noticed that Oscar and Cheddar were inching closer to Mac-Tavish. She wanted to shoo them back into the bathroom, but any motion on her part might end in that revolver going off.

Because she saw Cheddar every day Taylor hadn't noticed he was quite a large cat now. She knew tabbies tended to be stocky. Oscar was his usual sleek self, elegant in every way. The two of them were divergent creatures except for their love for her.

Cheddar was getting far too close to MacTavish for her liking, but she dared not say anything. Taylor received another message. The word *okay* showed up in her mind. It felt reassuring. She could swear it was coming from Cheddar. He looked right at her.

What happened in the next few minutes would be a life-long memory for Taylor and Jim. Cheddar reached MacTavish and viciously attacked his leg. Keeping his vice-like hold, the tabby sunk every available claw through his pants and into his flesh. Before MacTavish could react, Oscar ran shrieking as he jumped to MacTavish's shoulder biting him on the ear and scratching his head furiously. MacTavish dropped the gun denting her floor. It spun across the floor out of reach. MacTavish screamed as he flailed about trying to rid himself of Oscar. His arm slipped through the ladder. Within a few seconds he was tangled in the ladder Taylor had left out. She was secretly cheering for the ladder but terrified for her cats. He thrashed about within its rails and rungs and went down.

Afraid MacTavish would hurt her cats; Taylor jumped to her feet, grabbed the Zuni pot and broke it over his head. She was relieved to see him pass out. Maybe he'd be unconscious until Victor could get there.

The cats scattered in two directions; Cheddar scurried to hide behind Jim's chair while Oscar landed safely from a death-defying height and disappeared into the kitchen. One of his favorite hidey-holes was under the table on the banco.

Jim yanked out his belt. He securely tied MacTavish in a rather humiliating hog-tie. Taylor was ready to grab another pot if needed.

"Get Victor!" Jim was high on adrenaline.

Taylor picked up her phone. Her hands were shaking.

"Victor," she squeaked into the speaker.

"I heard," Victor said. "I'm turning into your driveway." He quickly notified dispatch to send officers to Taylor's house. By the time he got to her door, Taylor was holding it open.

"I thought you'd never get here," she said with relief. "But I'm so glad you are now." She wanted to hug him, but Victor was in detective mode and giving orders over his phone.

"Are you okay?" he asked roughly.

"Yes, come in, please"

He cuffed MacTavish, now alert, and read him his rights. In a few minutes there were cruisers and officers in her drive. A bloodied Mac-Tavish was packed into a vehicle and escorted to the police headquarters.

As officers and lab techs did their thing, Victor, Taylor and Jim congregated on her deck along with the two hero cats who placidly licked their fur back into place. From all appearances the cats were occupied with normal grooming. They were nonplused by the whole incident.

"I'm not clear what happened?" Victor said. "Suddenly there were cats yowling and sounds of things falling. Which one of you took him down?"

"It was Taylor's cats," Jim said.

Victor looked incredulous. "Say what?"

"Cheddar attacked his leg and Oscar flew through the air like a flying squirrel, landed on his shoulder and mercilessly scratched his head," Jim explained. "He was striking blows like a boxer only with claws. I've never seen anything like it. I think the two of them orchestrated their own hit."

Victor was astonished and looked to Taylor for confirmation.

"What he said. I couldn't be more proud had they graduated college."

Chapter 58

By Monday morning, everything seemed almost ordinary. Taylor and Jim joined everyone in the Piñon Publishing board room. Word of the fearless felines had made its way around the office. The water cooler network was in fine working order.

Taylor sat down beside Aponi. Jim took the available seat on Aponi's other side. The publishing crew awaited the arrival of Jessica. Candi removed her apparatus and turned on the answering system as Jessica descended the staircase.

Jessica flounced into the room. Today's outfit was royal blue, one of the best colors for television as she had done a couple of interviews this morning. Taylor had been asked but declined letting Jessica tell the story of her employees helping bring down a drug smuggling operation in Santa Fe County and beyond. She had been honest and included the mention of Taylor's and Jim's names, even going so far as to express her pride in their extracurricular activities.

At the lectern she leaned over. Everyone held their breath; an expensive lapis necklace languished on her chest. Finally, having cast her executive gaze on her underlings she came to the point.

"I'm happy to report that I, with Aponi's assistance, have secured loans to return to normal business, and yes, pay your full salaries plus the half-month you missed a few days ago. Those of you who work with our authors may tell them their books are now a go."

A cheer went up from the table.

"Okay, okay," Jessica admonished. "Candi, leave the answering system on and everyone take a two-hour lunch. Yes, you can consider it time paid."

"Is our fearless leader going soft?" Jim whispered

Taylor couldn't help but feel happy. It was moments like this she loved her job and co-workers; even Jessica.

"Now, get out of here, enjoy your lunch and be prepared to work when you return." She said sternly, in parting.

"Oh, there she is."

"Jim, really," Taylor said.

Aponi sitting between them smiled. She was starting to like working at the book publisher.

"Del Charro?" Jim asked.

"Of course," Taylor said.

"Would you like to join us for lunch?" Taylor asked Aponi.

"Do I have to solve a mystery?"

Taylor thought a moment. "You might want to sharpen your detective skills."

Epilogue

Edgar A. Perry's book was published on schedule; although he was a bit disappointed he had no reason to complain. Rebecca adopted Jethro. They have become fast friends and take long walks. The Wine and Crime book club reconvened with Rebecca Wilson now in the role of president. Their meetings have returned to pleasant conversation about books and of course plenty of wine and tea.

MacTavish is living it up at the New Mexico State Penitentiary. José Mendez was found dead in the shack where Barker had been held. The medical examiner reported he died of a snake bite. Taylor and Jim can't come to a conclusion as to what really happened in that cabin. Taylor believes Rachel Blackstone was correct in saying mysterious unexplained things happen in those woods. Jim will only say he saw a light.

José's two consorts were found deceased in the forest.

Gerald Barker closed El Jardín Encantado to regroup. He recovered from his ordeal and made a large donation to the local drug recovery group. No evidence indicated Barker had been involved in the wrong doing. Victor confirmed Anita was afraid of Barker because José worked for him.

The Mayan Death Pepper is in even greater demand.

Aponi is beginning to feel a part of the Piñon Publishing book world and looks forward to getting to know the crew. Jim is working on a new art exhibition. It promises to be even more successful than the last. Tom has become his faithful tabby companion. Taylor thinks that maybe the senior cat has inspired Jim to follow a new path. It's never too late.

Taylor is getting estimates for a burglar alarm and loving her life in Santa Fe, despite the strangely high murder rate. Oscar and Cheddar are still eating separately, but since their excursion into hoo-man protection they are taking a few naps together. But Taylor wonders if Cheddar has some special magic. She had saved his life; maybe he returned the favor. It was likely a one-time thing.

Anita remains officially missing. Juan Gonzáles continues to ride 63A every day looking for her. Taylor fears she may be another casualty of the Pecos Triangle.

If you drive a white Honda, please avoid Devil's Road. You are warned.

Author's Note

Publishing is a complex industry, at once creative and yet a business. The myriad of details that must be accomplished before a book can be published is difficult to comprehend, especially to the author waiting in the wings.

On average, an author will spend several months to a year writing a book. Whether traditionally or indie published, there are many decisions along the way: white or cream paper, gloss or matte cover, font choice and cover art. Marketing includes sales rep presentation, ARC (advance review copy; also referred to as a galley), choosing reviewers and requesting interviews. And then, there is the yearly trek to Book-Expo America for four days, presented by the American Booksellers Association. Steps to publication include editing, typesetting, blue-line, proofs and finally a book you can hold in your hands. It can take a year to publication unless the publisher fast tracks it because it's topical or urgent reading.

Daily life at a book publisher can range from deadly quiet to abject chaos, all the while processing the hundreds to thousands of manuscripts and queries that arrive daily. Today, more queries are submitted via email, but some writers still use the mail route. Envelopes and boxes holding the blood, sweat and tears of writers are stacked on desks, office floors, hallways and in closets. Most are returned unread by unpaid interns with a form letter and are never seen by editors.

Writers write because they must; because they have stories to tell. Make an author's day and write a short review describing why you liked – or loved their book. The next time you pick up a book, know it was a very long journey to your hands.

Acknowledgements

This book marks my first character crossover. Rachel Blackstone, Chloe Valdez and Mari-Lynn Alo of the Rachel Blackstone Paranormal Mystery series took time out from solving mysteries to help Taylor Browning discover Santa Fe's inexplicable side.

My thanks to my lifemate who acted as my first reader for years and continues to brainstorm with me over dinner and drinks while I'm writing down ideas as fast as I can hoping my meal doesn't get cold.

Much appreciation to my friends who support and encourage me: Cheryl, Judi, Marilyn ... Barbara, Helen, Sharon, Susan, Terry and Willow.

To Santa Fe, New Mexico, a city rich in history and three cultures, for providing a beautiful and intriguing background.

Del Charro Saloon is a real restaurant in Santa Fe, found in the Inn of the Governors. It is popular with both visitors and locals. Located on the corner of West Alameda and Don Gaspar, you can watch the world go by or catch the score while enjoying food and margaritas. Psst. Their green chile is wonderful!

For more information on Devil's Road

For the history of Devil's Road and tours of Santa Fe, go to Allan Pacheco's website at:

https://www.santafeghostandhistorytours.com/NEW-MEXICO-MISSING.html

He also does a fascinating ghost tour!

About the Author

GG Collins once worked for a book publisher, before she walked a reporter's beat. Take this experience; add a mystery, a feline companion, great friends and a new cozy mystery series is born.

Collins has been cat mom to a baker's dozen, all with their own eccentricities. Somehow, they end up as pets in her books. Oscar is the reincarnation of her late Abyssinian cat. The character of Cheddar is inspired by her beloved orange tabby. She also loves and writes about horses.

Book Blog:
https://reluctantmediumatlarge.wordpress.com

News, Views & Reviews Blog:
https://paralleluniverseatlarge.wordpress.com